Advance Praise for Street Disciples & Isaiah David Paul

"*Street Disciples* is a tale filled with wonderful characters that are facing demons that have infiltrated their lives.

It's a powerful story of people gaining strength to battle life's trials and tribulations in search of redemption and peace. Isaiah David Paul has chosen an array of colorful characters in this humbling story, and I won't be surprised if you find a bit of yourself within the pages."

--Barbara Grovner
Author of the *COLD* series

"Isaiah David Paul's style is edgy and breathtaking, yet elegant."
--BNTasty 1
Author of *Life of an Ex College Bandsmen IV: Wedding Bells*

"Isaiah David Paul will have you turning pages."
--Mike Sanders
Author of *Thirsty 1 & 2, Hustlin' Backwards* and *Snitch*

broken
but i'm
healed

broken but i'm healed

Isaiah David Paul

10'sLee Phelps

www.writesingwork.com
a literary entertainment company

□Winston-Salem ▪ Denver ▪ Atlanta □

10's Lee Phelps & Write Sing Work titles are published by Write Sing Work, LLC, 6255 Towncenter Drive #1669, Clemmons, North Carolina 27012

Based on the short story, "I Used To Love H.E.R" by Jarold Imes as published in *The Soul of a Man* Edited by Elissa Gabrielle. Published by Peace in the Storm Publishing. ISBN 0-9819631-3-7. Copyright 2007 Jarold Imes. Used by permission. All Rights Reserved.

Book Credits
Author & Cover Designer: Jarold Imes writing as Isaiah David Paul for Write Sing Work, LLC
Associate Editors: Barbara S. Grovner, Lorraine Elzia, Elissa Gabrielle for Peace in the Storm Publishing and Bethany Hamilton Freebird
Photograph: Corbis

16 15 14 13 12 11 10 9 8 7

Scripture taken from the New King James Version. Copyright © 1982 by Thomas Nelson, Inc. Used by permission. All rights reserved.

Scripture also taken from the Revised Standard Version of the Bible, copyright 1952 [2nd edition, 1971] by the Division of Christian Education of the National Council of the Churches of Christ in the United States of America. Used by permission. All rights reserved.

ISBN 13: 978-1-934195-82-6/ISBN 10: 1-934195-82-0 (print)
ISBN 13: 978-1-934195-57-4/ISBN 10: 1-934195-57-X (eBook)

The model or models and/or image or images on the cover is a visualization of the story and are not intended to portray any characters or localizations in the book. The photographer and/or models were solicited and compensated for their participation.

Printed in the United States of America & Canada

In memory of...

For a time in my life, I was lucky. After years of begging, I finally got another Big Bro. In the short time I was blessed to be in his presence, I learned everything I needed to know about survival. He taught me love, grace, patience and most importantly, how to survive being "thirty." And to think that if he could make it in the position that he was in, that I no longer had a right to complain about my life's ups and downs.

Thanks Mas...for the simplest of life's lessons. If it's the Lord's will, we will get to walk around heaven—and I'll read *Where the Wild Things Are* to you.

1981 - 2012

dedication

For every man and woman who's made it their life's mission to educate a generation where adults aren't respected and teachers are blamed for everything. Remember, I used to be in front of the classroom, too. I know how hard it is. Maybe one day, we can lobby congress for better support of the good teachers instead of making reality shows for those who don't deserve the title. Remember God's judgment for the teachers...

I learned...

Chapter One

Early Sunday Morning, November 7, 2010
Grace United Methodist Church—Before Service
Winston-Salem, North Carolina

"Heavenly Father—please don't send me to hell for sleeping with my ex-wife…again." Calvin repented as he backed his car into his favorite spot on the other end of the church property. Only two parking spaces separated him from the brand new trash can and recycling bins the church got after the parking lot had just been paved the week before. The traditional markings were the same.

Calvin cut off the ignition and looked down at his platinum wedding band. The divorce was final a year ago and he still wore it as if he said "I do" yesterday. He twisted the ring on his finger with his thumb. *It's because you haven't let her go,* the voice inside him spoke. Calvin could decipher the Spirit's conviction almost instantly. And it was right, Calvin found it hard to let Maria go, even after she cheated on him and he caught her in a series of lies about her infidelity that led to their divorce.

"Naw, I haven't let her go," Calvin confessed. Calvin agreed to meet with Maria two days ago. He took her up on an offer to get out of town and go sightseeing. In their short trip down I-40, Calvin and Maria experienced a level of intimacy they'd never shared during the five years they were married. In Durham, they'd spent time shopping, eating, and sightseeing. A few more miles down the road in Raleigh caught them spending some quality time with one another. Raleigh proved to be a good escape from their life in Winston.

Upon returning from their short trip, Calvin and Maria pretended they were back in their younger days. They hastily made a return to the marriage bed that legally, and in God's eyes, no longer existed.

"God, sometimes when Maria and I get together, I get confused because we stood before You and said we would stay together, and remain faithful to one another until death do us part. But the State of North Carolina parted us because *she* didn't want to be married no more; *she* wanted to be with another man."

Calvin's mind turned to thoughts of Maria's smooth bronze-colored skin that felt like cool Jell-O butterscotch pudding. An irony at times, her touch was as cold as an icebox. "Now I'm the other man; I'm playing the role of the man I despised."

Calvin was about to step out of the car. He grabbed his Bible and his small backpack that contained copies of the current issues of *The Upper Room* that his ministry group, the Street Disciples distributed and sold. He opened the tattered and worn Bible to pull out a note on some verses he needed clarification on and his eyes were glued to the verse, *blessed is the man who endures temptation; for when he has been approved, he will receive the crown of life which the Lord has promised to those who love Him.*

The twelfth verse in the first chapter of James was right and Calvin sat up, feeling like a fool. "God, I trust and pray one day I will have the strength not to go on like this," he prayed as he made his way out of the car. He reached in his pocket and locked the door using the keyless remote and headed toward the door of the lobby.

God, You said in Your word that if I repented with my whole heart that my sins would be forgiven. I trust You to do that and to give me the strength to resist the temptation the next time it arises. Calvin thought of these words as he stepped through the doors. Immediately he'd heard compliments on his dark gray Sean Jean suit, which was highlighted with a bright, neon blue button up that he managed to acquire on the trip to Raleigh. The matching black Stacy Adams dress shoes was a comfortable choice, and he was glad he'd chosen them. He shook hands and hugged the other parishioners, as he made his way to a small room two doors down from the sanctuary. There, he removed his suit jacket, revealing dark gray suspenders and a blue and gray diamond tie that completed the look he was going for. Calvin was surprised to see the television on, but decided he'd catch a few minutes of a Dr. Bobby Jones interview with an up and coming gospel act before Sunday school was to start. His spirit was at ease.

"All right gentlemen, we're going to talk about repentance." Calvin heard his older brother, Carlton command the attention of the others whom were in the room. He stared at his lighter-reflection and smiled at the fact that they nearly had the same taste in suits…save for Carlton's was black and he wore green where Calvin had blue.

Calvin knew that once Carlton got started, God was going to reveal a message specifically for him. He pulled out a highlighter from his pants pocket, traced the verse. He was anxious to receive the Word.

Chapter Two

Sunday Afternoon, November 7, 2010
Central YMCA – Street Disciples Ministry Outreach
Winston-Salem, North Carolina

"To God be the glory," Carlton said as he and other members of the Street Disciples Ministry Group were finishing their reps on the various workout machines in the weight room at the Y.

Calvin looked at his older brother in his black South Pole hoodie and matching cargo sweat pants, a sharp contrast from his attire that could've easily made him a model in the JCPenny's catalog. As other members of the group were sporting workout attire, it was painfully obvious that the dress code was casual, and that Calvin had forgotten they would be going to the gym to minister the city's lost souls.

Calvin stood out in his heavy black work shoes, black and green swimming trunks and lime green and white Sean Jean polo. Unlike the Stacy Adams he had on before, the SAFETRAX slip resistance shoes would be uncomfortable for walking long periods of time.

"Bro, I tried to call you last night, where were you?" Carlton questioned as he took a seat next to Calvin at the bench press.

"Some place I shouldn't have been." Calvin knew that his lack of ability to put together something more presentable would start something with his brother sooner or later, and now was just as good a time as any.

Carlton stepped to Calvin, took a couple of sniffs and chuckled. "You and Maria get married again?"

"Shut up," Calvin mumbled back.

"I wish I could marry my ex-wife every time the temptation hit."

Calvin scowled and he was tempted to forget that he and the man sitting next to him had the same parents.

"Cartlon, be nice."

Calvin turned around to see Rahliem Victor, leader of the ministry walk toward him. Even with the towel over his shoulder, the netted tank top only concealed some of the tattoos that were on his arms from an earlier prison stint. The massive artwork spanned from the top of his neck, down the length of both arms, and covered his torso and back. His wedding band sparkled. Calvin looked down at his own left hand and found that he still had his ring on.

"Everyone falls short of the glory of God from time to time," Rahliem reminded everyone as he sat down to work on the exercise bike.

Calvin nodded his head as he saw Donte and his son, Eugene take a seat near the back. Calvin remembered when Eugene used to cling to his father and wished that he had a son that would do that. He could hear Eugene counting the reps his father was doing.

"The important thing is for us to repent and get back on track," Rahliem encouraged as he picked up his pace.

"It's difficult," Calvin spoke up. He wasn't about to let the lay leader of his church and his older brother gang up on him. "But I'm determined to see a better future…the one God designed for me. That is the only way I get through the next hour sometimes."

"I face the same problem," D had stated.

Daniel Abriel Jackson aka "D" was a young teenage father, having three children by the age of seventeen. D found God and joined Grace United Methodist Church after witnessing the work being done in his older brother, Chase. D became active with the Street Disciples Ministry, working to spread the word of God to other teenagers at his school and the For Father's Only ministry which the group had become affiliated with.

"Let me guess," Carlton was on a roll, "you still sleeping with Nachelle?"

"I don't understand," D complained as he stopped cycling, "there's a reason why we didn't have any more children after we had my first child. We fight like cats and dogs," D complained.

"That's usually how it starts," Calvin mumbled.

"So you admit it?" Carlton badgered.

"Get you an ex-wife and see how well you do," Calvin challenged.

"Look," Rahliem was being the rational one again. He slowed his pace as he faced Calvin. "I can't sit here and condone what you and D are doing. As long as there is no ring on the finger and no commitment to God, or if that commitment is broken, then sleeping with your ex-wife, ex-girlfriend or whomever, is a sin."

Calvin looked down at the ring he was still wearing.

"That doesn't count Calvin, and there is no commitment behind that," Rahliem picked up the speed.

It was as if Rahliem had read his mind.

"Have you ever had pre-marital sex?" D directed toward Rahliem.

The room almost was quiet. Nosy Nancys and busy bodies wanted to hear if the great man of God would confess to this sin. For some, it would be the juiciest piece of gossip they'd get to spread all year. Rahliem had amassed status as the favorite guest speaker and respected religious leader. Could he have been as perfect as the Word he professed to following?

"Yes, I've had premarital sex. I did some things before I went to jail and fell short after my stint." Rahliem admitted—no shame or guilt in his voice. "But I'm not proud of it. I wish my first time was with my wife and I wish that prison turned out differently. But it happened, I repented and now I'm only seeking that level of comfort with my wife."

Calvin felt a sense of conviction he'd never felt before. It wasn't that he took joy in lusting and living a fantasy every time he and Maria connected. "I know why I sleep with Maria."

"Why?" Carlton interrogated and pressed for more information.

"Comfort," Calvin confessed. Didn't take much to break him. "Maria and I were married for five years and been dating since I was sixteen. I know her body as well as I know my own. I trust her in the bedroom and I'm comfortable with her. After all, in the eyes of God, we are still married."

"No you're not," Rahliem wanted to snap. Calvin could see Rahliem trying to contain his temper. "You are not married. Once the judge declared you divorced and you rightfully filed for divorce because she committed adultery...in God's eyes you are no longer married. But the fact that you are sleeping with her even though she's with the man that she committed adultery with, is what makes you wrong. In God's eyes, you're sleeping with her, and Bilal's sleeping with her, makes you both sinners. You are just as much of an adulterer as he is...and as I was."

"I sleep with Nachelle for comfort too," D admitted. "We argue so much about everything. The kids, my other baby mamas, child support, my hours at my job. Make up sex seems to be the only way we know how to make up. And we'd be cool for a while until she starts tripping."

"Naw, you sleep with her because the other two baby's mamas cut you off," Carlton answered honestly. D had his head down, which also confirmed that what was said was the truth.

"Carlton, that was not nice and you can't go tit for tat with these dudes like we used to do when we were in the pen,"

Rahliem admonished him. "We are here not only for a physical work out but a spiritual one too. I bared my soul not to brag about my sins, but to show you and others who were listening how transparent our ministry is. We are not a holier than thou association, we are a group of men, God's men, who have fallen short, and have come back to work and encourage others to do the same."

"That's why I'm here," D testified. "I've fallen and gotten back up many times with no judgment from anyone. I can still come to Rahliem or Donte or Celtius or even you two knuckleheads and read the word. And, I've been broken but I'm healed here too," D testified.

"Hey brothers," they were interrupted by a slender young man with a baby face.

"Robert, what's going on?" Rahliem got up and gave him a hug.

"I'm hanging in there. Sorry I'm late," the soft-spoken man responded. Robert looked at all of the men in the room and smiled.

"No, you're okay. We're working out our bodies and our problems."

"Good, I'm done backsliding and I'm looking to be with like-minded individuals who are willing to help me stick with my goals."

Robert stopped talking. Everyone noticed the black and Asian mixed man he was looking at as he was walking with another, taller, light skinned guy.

"Aurice," Rahliem addressed the light skinned guy.

"Trouble," Aurice cracked back as he looked down at the shorter man. Rahliem shook his head.

"Aye, this is my roommate Cedric. Cedric, this is the infamous Rahliem Victor. He's the leader of the Street Disciple Ministry I was telling you about."

Rahliem introduced Calvin, Carlton, D, Donte and Eugene. The men shook hands and began working out in close proximity.

"I didn't know you knew Aurice," Robert was noticeably uncomfortable when he and Cedric shared glances.

"Aurice and I went to school together. He was trying to get me on the straight and narrow in back then, but I had too many anger management issues. Right now, he's working with teens with behavior issues and he's active in his church. I know Pastor Goodwill, he's a good man."

"Well, I'm going to catch you later," Robert gathered his stuff quickly and walked away. Carlton scrunched his lips and was as confused as Calvin was.

"Rah, what was that all about?" Carlton looked between Robert and Cedric and still couldn't figure it out.

"Everyone has things they must leave behind and I trust Robert is doing what he must," Rahliem advised.

Calvin shook his head, "I need to have the same kind of will power that Robert has."

"You will be tested again and every test will build up the power you need to resist the temptation that will come in many forms. The question is, are you willing to receive that power?"

Calvin shook his head yes. It wasn't like he and Maria had sex often but when they did, he couldn't get enough. He wanted to reconcile but knew that wasn't the best option.

Until Calvin could figure something out, he was going to have to find a way to resist Maria's temptation.

Chapter Three

Saturday, November 20, 2010
Japanese Steakhouse
Winston-Salem, North Carolina

"No Bilal, I will *not* marry you!" Maria vowed before putting a forkful of hibachi bananas in her mouth. As she chewed her food fast, the chef serving them accidentally dropped the chopping tool and the whole place had become silent.

Bilal Kodjoe quickly lifted his lanky, toothpick-thin frame from off his knee and took his seat next to her. He shifted his body to face her instead of the chef, who continued to perform circus tricks with the food he was preparing for the other patrons.

"What'd you just say?" Bilal was in denial, having heard her the first time and instead of placing the two karat ring on her finger, he left the black box that he'd just picked up from Kay's Jeweler on the table. "I asked you if you would marry me." Bilal looked around and he could see every man, woman, boy and girl looking at him. Some of the patrons had pity because they'd heard the rejection first time. Others were in shock because they couldn't believe he had the gall to ask again.

"I said, *no Bilal, I will not marry you…*" Maria quickly wiped her face with the cloth napkin that had been provided for her and noticed that some of her blackberry lipstick had made a permanent imprint on the cloth. "I can't believe you just asked me that."

Annoyed, Maria got up and walked as fast as her four inch stilettos would allow. Bilal quickly took out a Benjamin and slammed it on the table, leaving behind a half a bottle of saki and the vegetable teriyaki plate that he'd planned on boxing up to go. The food could wait. Bilal caught up with Maria right before she could get into the driver's side of her pearl-colored 1988 Mercury Cougar.

Maria opened the door and Bilal quickly slammed it shut. His face was turning red, rivaling the shade of a candied apple. His struggle with his feelings and his ability to contain his composure became evident as the seconds flew by like a ferry in a river.

"I can't believe you just embarrassed me like that in front of all of those people." Bilal's voice caught a frog. As he coughed, he found that the amphibian wouldn't let go. "I bought this ring, paid for this car. And not only are you rejecting my marriage proposal, you have the audacity to try to leave me in this parking lot."

"Look, I don't have time for this," Maria tried to open the door again but Bilal's lanky frame betrayed the strength he used to keep the door in its place. "What do you want from me?"

"I want to know the work I was putting into this relationship was not in vain."

"I just got a divorce."

"That I paid for!" Bilal's face was smoking and like a balloon, he was getting ready to pop. "I paid for the lawyer…I paid for the court costs…I'm paying for the condo you're staying in."

Maria hauled off and smacked him, instantly changing the roles in their situation and regaining her pimp status. "I don't owe you an explanation. And just because you paid some rinky-dink lawyers to play presto-change-o on a piece of paper in some office doesn't mean you got papers on me. And why would I want to marry you anyway? You don't even know me."

"And how could I not know you? You've been in my bed. We've shared our dreams and our secrets, we…" his voice trailed off.

"So because we tell each other bedtime stories and party like rock stars, you think that makes us best friends?" Maria rolled her eyes before walking around the car and getting in on the passenger's side. Bilal followed and turned on the ignition and forced his seat belt buckle to latch. "You don't even remember how I lost my virginity do you?"

Bilal forcefully exhaled. He knew he would have to continue to show his love for her. Make her a believer. He'd have to boost her self-esteem. The frustration of having a strong, Brazilian woman at his side as he looked to start his new church in the next year were beginning to fade like rain from a window pane. "Yes, I remember how you lost your virginity." Bilal stated calmly.

"You remember?"

"Yes, I remember!" He lost his patience.

Maria looked at him, rolled her eyes and stared out the window as Bilal finally made it onto Silas Creek Parkway to head toward his apartment near Wake Forest University. "Tell it to me." She turned off the high energy Tye Tribbett song—not feeling the victory he and his choir were singing about. "Tell it to me right now!"

Bilal slowed his car to the stop light near Forsyth Technical Community College. At the last minute he decided to turn onto the vacant campus and find a parking space.

"You were a little girl in Brazil, in a small village outside of Goiânia."

"Yeah, yeah, yeah, I know that part."

"Maria can you let me finish!"

"Go ahead."

"Like I was saying, you were about to turn twelve in the village of…"

Bilal started a story he knew all too well, and the thought of the nightmares he'd wake Maria up from. As the next words flowed from his lips, Maria's childhood came to life.

Chapter Four

Tuesday, October 30, 1984
Maria's Childhood Home
Goiânia, Brazil

Maria held onto her only sister's hand as they made their way to their home. She was determined not to let the taunting from the other quasi-rich kids in the neighborhood get under her skin.

"Maria, why are they calling our mother a slut?" Avia was in tears.

Maria looked down at her little sister. She did not want to believe that the eight year old could fathom such a question. An eight year old who had no business saying, let alone being able to define what a *slut* was.

"Maria..." Avia whined.

"I heard you, I heard you," Maria tried not to yell too loud. The taunting grew louder and louder and became too much for Maria to bear. "They just think they know things about our mother but they know nothing at all."

Maria was happy when they finally made it to their house at the bottom of the hill. She smiled inwardly to herself when one of the girls who'd been taunting her got snatched up like a rag doll and firmly disciplined in front of their peers. The attention turned from them to the "bad girl" and gave the mean kids someone else to laugh at and pick on for a change.

Maria was getting ready to pull her key out of her pocket and she looked at the driveway again. Their father's government-issued car was parked unusually in the driveway—he was supposed to be at work. Almost immediately, Maria began to think the worst but decided that whatever it was, would be something that could be fixed.

"Daddy's home!" Avia screamed excitedly as she danced at her sister's side. "Hurry up, I want to see daddy."

"Calm down," Maria stopped intentionally. She waited until her sister got her bearings together and once she was satisfied, she put the key back in the lock. "Look, we are going to go to the table and sit down. Eat a light snack and do our homework first before you go play outside."

"What if Daddy gets the maid to do it?"

"Liza will not be doing your homework tonight." Maria exhaled and shook her head. She was disappointed because she had this conversation with Avia before. "Besides, one day, you are going to be the wife of someone very powerful and the last thing whomever you are blessed to marry will need is a dumb little girl who doesn't know her alphabet and her numbers."

Maria looked at Avia. She decided to ignore her sister as she pouted then opened the door and watched Avia go through her usual routine of taking her shoes off at the door and then head to the cupboard to pull out a packaged fruit cookie snack and then sit at the table. Maria locked the door behind her and repeated the action of her sister.

"Thank you."

Avia stuck her tongue out at her and rolled her eyes. *My sister is so spoiled*, Maria thought as she walked to the table to get her own snack. Just as she was about to take a step into the kitchen, she heard a noise in their back room.

"Padre?" She called out but instead of seeing a short, well-built man with a thick mustache with bald hair, she saw a man in his early thirties who looked like one of the track stars on the Jamaican Olympic Team. His raisin colored complexion shined on his bald crown. The man reminded Maria of a black Mr. Clean and though very sculpted in build, not so much that he'd draw a Mr. T comparison. The licorice colored eyes commanded attention.

"Hello young lady," the dark man stood before her. "Are you and your sister okay?"

"Who are you?" Maria questioned, thinking the worst. In the back of her mind, she remembered the numerous kidnappings that had taken place in the last couple of weeks. American children had their faces plastered on posters and milk cartons. South American children were broadcast on the radio and pleas from European parents could be seen on BBC and other news outlets. She was praying that she and Avia wouldn't be next.

"I am Dr. Markel Alvarez—I'm a good friend of your father's and I've come to take you and your sister with me to the Dominican Republic." Before Maria could scream, Dr. Alvarez rushed behind her and put his hand over her lips. He picked up the young lady and he carried her to her father's room. "I do not come to bring you harm, but I want you to know that your father is not well and your mother's boyfriend and his goons are coming for the two of you to sell you to some slave traders."

Dr. Alvarez opened the door and Maria could see her beloved father resting peacefully. He pulled out a Beta cassette and put it in the player above the television.

"My dearest Maria and Avia," Maria saw her father on the screen. "If you are watching this, then you know that I am either dead or on my deathbed."

Maria let out a light shrill and tears fell from her face.

"The man, who gives you this tape is named Dr. Markel Alvarez—one of my most dearest friends. If you need to check his identity, look for his picture in my family album."

Maria made a move to the dresser and grabbed it from the spot on the lower shelf where she remembered seeing it last. She scanned through the pages and saw a younger version of Dr. Alvarez and her father hanging out in San Francisco de Campeche, Mexico. Maria had been a couple of times in her youth. She had always known that her father was half-Mexican, but it was a fact that was rarely talked about. Her father's rise as a successful investment broker who made his clients millions of dollars made the fact that he was a non-native of Brazil a moot point.

"My friend has been instructed to take the two of you to a safe house in Bienvenido, a small town outside of the capital of the Dominican Republic. His family will place you in a good school and make sure that you two are prepared for the life I wanted to provide for you.

"The rumors you've heard about the status of my marriage to your mother are true—and for that I'm sorry. I'm sure she's gone on to be with Mayor Sangrieo and they are somewhere enjoying a life without me and the two of you. I'm sorry that I won't be around long enough to see you get married or have children. But do know that I'm thinking of you, and that I have prayed that God will watch over you on earth and that our Heavenly Father has mercy on me."

The short message confused Maria, but before she could think straight, Dr. Alvarez grabbed her and dragged her to her room. He looked in her closet and grabbed the suitcase and tossed it at her. "Only pack what you can carry. You are not safe here." Dr. Alvarez began tossing some clothes in the suitcase. "We only have fifteen minutes to get in and get out."

Maria decided not to argue with the man. She grabbed two school uniforms, three shirts and pants and as much underwear as she could pack. Maria looked around her room one last time, and then rushed out, promising herself that she would cherish her memories.

"I got your sister's bag already. I also packed a bag lunch because we got a long drive before we get on the plane. We can't fly out of the country from here."

Maria just shook her head and followed Dr. Alvarez. Avia was asking a hundred questions that Dr. Alvarez pretended not to hear as he carried her and her bag to the car. Maria stared back at her and couldn't help but feel sad because not only was she leaving her dead father behind, she had a strong feeling that she'd never see her mother again.

Chapter Five

"And shortly after that, Dr. Alvarez molested you in a hotel room before taking you to Mexico."

Maria looked at Bilal and shook her head. She exhaled. "Dr. Alvarez was not the one who raped me you idiot."

"So who did? Every time you tell the story, you always imply that Dr. Alvarez was the one who did it."

Maria opened her mouth to speak and a loud tapping noise could be heard against her window pane. They both faced the cop who was standing outside in the light rain. Maria rolled down her window. "Is there a problem officer?"

"There was a report of illicit activity. Is everything okay?"

"Yeah, we're fine. We just needed to sort some things out."

"Alright no problem. Unfortunately, I'm going to have to ask you to leave the premises. We don't want anyone to accuse you of doing something you aren't doing."

Maria started the car while Bilal squinted his eyes. He didn't like the way the police officer was implying that he and Maria were having sex in the car. He reached inside his coat jacket and pulled out the small pocket size book of Psalms and Proverbs and turned to a random page. "I can't believe you said no to me." Bilal mumbled under his lips.

"How about I tell you the rest of the story one last time?" Maria got on Silas Creek Parkway and then she began to tell him the part of the story she rarely told anyone before.

Chapter Six

Friday, November 2, 1984
Guerrilla Compound
Juarez, Mexico

It had been days since Maria had seen Dr. Alvarez. After he was shot in his chest and left to die in the car, a band of guerrilla warriors had taken Maria and Avia from his car outside of Goiânia and smuggled them along with some other children to a port city in Mexico. They, along with four other children from the Caribbean and South America had been kept in the house for the last twenty four hours to be cleaned and inspected so they could be photographed and sold to perspective buyers in the United States and Europe.

The guerrilla warriors' plans had been foiled as they were involved in a war outside the home. Maria, Avia and all the other children were split up and Maria sought safety in an underground shelter. She had no idea where Avia or the other children were and she remembered falling to sleep twice since she had been in the shelter. Her stomach seemed to be twisted in knots and she felt like she could no longer taste her saliva.

Maria was hungry—she wanted something to eat. But she had no idea what she was going to eat or where she was going to get it from.

Her reservation was that she didn't know what danger awaited her once she lifted the door from her shelter. The gunshots had disappeared hours ago and she didn't know whether to trust the silence or to be cautious. Maria knew she would die if she didn't get something to eat soon—but she also knew that if she weren't careful—a misaligned bullet or a forceful hand could mean the death of her anyway.

Maria lifted the door and the foul stench attacked her full force. Her captor faced her with part of his dome leaking from the gunshot wound that had taken his life. She wanted to hurl, but had nothing to expel.

Suddenly, Maria felt her body being snatched up and as she looked around, her desire and craving for food decreased. Her captor's body was one of many that had lain dead—many of the bodies belonging to children whom she didn't know were in the area. As she made her way up, she caught the attention of a sand colored man with bushy eyebrows and a thick mustache.

"Where are the rest of the children?" He asked her in broken English. Maria hated speaking English but knew that she had to rely on her school lessons if she thought to make it out alive.

"I—don't know." She answered.

Five fingers and a palm roughly met with her face and turned her head sideways. "You do know."

"I don't know—I promise."

The man sent one of his soldiers into the shelter and moments later, he came up to confirm Maria's story. The man who grabbed her, tossed her over his shoulders like a rag doll. She looked around as they ran out of the building. Maria couldn't find a trace of Avia nowhere and she decided at that moment that there was no way on earth she would betray her sister if somehow, she had been able to escape.

Maria knew that her life was changing and that this moment in time, she'd never forget.

Chapter Seven

"And later that day—a twelve year old girl got a taste of what it is like to be a woman."

Maria shed tears for the first time in what seemed to be a lifetime. She looked out of the window and saw the condo. She looked at the newly painted white building and then she looked back at Bilal. She realized that she was staring at the only other man beside her father and her ex-husband that she truly loved.

"So you still want to marry me?" Maria looked at her neighbor pulling into his parking space. "You know that I will never believe in your God or fulfill your dream of being first lady of the church you want to build."

"I'm not asking you to be any of these things for me. I'm just saying marry me—and open your heart and be receptive to the fact that God can heal and change all matters in your life. Jesus is the way, the truth and the light—he can't heal you if you don't let him in."

"I don't want to," Maria mumbled through her tears.

"Why don't you want to give Jesus a chance?"

Maria opened the door and then she slammed it. She didn't care whether or not Bilal got up and followed her or not. Maria heard Bilal approaching her but decided not to stop. "If Jesus were real—then how come *I* had to go through all of that? How come those men raped me? How come I was a sex slave until I was fifteen? How come the first baby I had got murdered and I've never been able to conceive with Calvin? If Jesus is real—and he really loved me—wouldn't Jesus know and realize that I've been through enough?"

"Testimony," Bilal answered.

"But I don't want to testify. I want to be healed."

"My God is Jehovah Raphe, the great healer."

"Yeah, your God also said thou shalt not commit adultery and you had no problem helping me do that."

Bilal rolled his eyes. He hated how people always seemed to twist the Bible to make a situation fit them. Instead of following her to her condo, he turned around and decided to walk the half mile back to his place and leave Maria to her thoughts. He was tired of fighting this battle with her and decided that he had another day to help win Maria's salvation.

Chapter Eight

Sunday, November 20, 2010
Maria's Condo
Winston-Salem, North Carolina

Maria was stressed. Bilal's proposal came completely out of left field. She tried to enjoy the movie *Welcome Home Roscoe Jenkins* with Martin Lawrence and Cedric the Entertainer, but she just couldn't get into the "Team of Me." She turned the volume down on her flat screen to flip the pages of TuShonda Whitaker's *Millionaire Wives Club*—getting into the sassy and sophisticated characters of reality television into the palm of her hands but the knocking on her door to be a nuisance.

"Every time I try to get something done, someone's always messing with me."

Between her unwelcome visitor pounding on her door as if they were a member of the S.W.A.T. team and her neighbor's erotically charged music featuring a female talking about the things she can do invading the privacy of her home, Maria was frustrated. She grabbed the remote and turned the volume up.

Maria flipped another page on her book and was getting back into the drama. A part of her wished she could live in the world where they lived and her pain and suffering be forgotten.

"Maria, you alright." The familiar voice yelled after her.

Maria was startled when she turned around. She looked Calvin Rice in the eyes. Her heart jumped into her throat as she was trying to figure out how he got into her condo. There stood her ex-husband in a Carolina blue muscle shirt and matching jersey shorts. She loved how the color complimented his pancake-colored skin tone.

"You left your keys in the door and after knocking for a few minutes, I let myself in to check on you."

Maria smiled. She loved looking at Calvin's full lips and light brown eyes. As she lowered her eyes, she noticed that his pecs seemed to bounce as he breathed—the eight-pack was perfect. The music in the background only added to the lust as she focused on his midsection and licked her lips at his legs that sculpted as if Usain Bolt had trained them for his record-breaking one hundred millimeter dash. She wanted to forget that she and the man she was in lust with weren't married and pretend that they were for a few moments.

"I'm fine," Maria insisted. "What brings you by?" She quickly looked on the end table and found the laminated obituary of her mother that she was using as a bookmark and place it in the book.

"Believe it or not, I was coming to check on you. I called a couple of times today but I—" Calvin decided not to answer as he let himself into her place, closing the door behind him.

Maria felt her heart beating faster as he took a seat next to her. She looked at the man and she noticed the scar that was near his left eye—a gift from the brother of the young man he killed when he was twelve. The way it twitched let her know that Calvin had a lot on his mind.

"So how do you like being engaged to Bilal?" Calvin asked as he turned to face her.

"He told you we were engaged?"

"No—he asked me if he had my blessing to marry you." Calvin chuckled as he noticed the still picture on the scene. "After all this time that the two of you were messing around, the last thing I'd expected him to do was to ask *my* permission for the two of you to tie the knot." Calvin rubbed his hands against his pants. "It felt awkward."

Maria shook her head—she couldn't believe that after all this time, she finally gotten this brother to break a sweat. "I didn't say yes."

"You might as well—at least you won't be living in sin."

Maria got up, her feelings hurt. "And what do you call what we did two weeks ago?"

"A mistake that won't happen again once you become Mrs. Bilal Kodjoe."

As much as Maria wanted to be mad at Calvin, she couldn't bring herself to say a foul word to him. At first, Maria hadn't felt bad about how she cheated on Calvin and often patted herself on the back for being blessed for having two of the finest men in her world fight, vie and underhand one another for her attention.

Maria often admitted to herself that she thought sex with Calvin was better after they divorced. Not that they had a regular relationship, but the few times she found comfort in his arms—for those few moments—she regretted leaving. Maria started to rub on his arm, hoping to initiate some contact but Calvin gently removed her hand from him and scooted over a few inches to put some space between them.

"As tempting as it is to get familiar with you again, I came over here mainly to say congratulations and that I wished you and Bilal the best and God's blessings if it is in His will."

"There you go with that God crap again." Maria snatched the remote from the table, pressed play and turned the volume all the way up.

At that moment, she remembered why she started cheating on Calvin. When he got saved, he tried in vain to get Maria to go to church and to worship God with him. That and their inability to have children that lived kept breaking their hearts and tearing them apart.

Calvin got up and walked in front of the television and turned it off. "God crap?" He said as he gritted at her. "My savior is bigger than the waste you've tried to reduce him to."

"Look, I don't want to argue with you. In a few days, I'm going to marry Bilal and if all you came to do was to tell me that you and I couldn't have sex anymore then fine—I won't miss it anyway."

Calvin rolled his eyes at her and that made her even madder. Truth was, she wanted Calvin to be available to her some of the time while she was with Bilal—just as things had been before.

"In a few days, you are going to marry a man of God." Calvin started. "A man who despite his flaws is after God's own heart—how can you not give his God—*our* God a chance?"

"Because I don't want to and I'm tired of having this conversation with you." Maria got up to and walked to the door to open in so that Calvin would leave. "We are done."

"No we're not—come back here and have a seat."

"I'm not your woman."

"And I'm not your man but that didn't stop you from going for broke a few minutes ago."

Maria hated when Calvin was right—in her mind she was always right. "Look—why don't we just get our few minutes in for the last time and call it a night."

"Aight." Calvin surprised her. "But first, before I take my clothes off, I want to explain to you how I've been feeling and how I've changed as a man."

Maria slammed the door and took a seat next to Calvin. Maria wanted her ex-husband for one last roll in the hay and was willing to do whatever to speed up the process. "Talk."

"I think I know where we went wrong with in our marriage. And if you want to have a better marriage with Bilal than you had with me, then you need to not make the same mistakes with him as you did with me."

"I don't make mistakes."

"Nobody's perfect. We had our issues and I think they got worse once I took that teaching job."

Maria's mind took a flashback to a time when Calvin was in graduate school and driving an hour back and forth from their apartment to his school in Concord. She remembered his school days like they were yesterday.

...this lesson...

Chapter Nine

Friday, June 6, 2008
Butler J. Parker High School
Concord, North Carolina
2:25 PM

The young, hip and energetic student broadcaster was going over the announcements concerning the upcoming exam schedule, study tips and graduation details for the Class of 2008 just minutes before the school bell rang. Once his announcement was over, the voice of Shannon Parris, the school secretary could be heard over the intercom.

"Mr. Rice and Mrs. Fieldtag, you are needed after school for a parent-teacher conference. Again, Mr. Rice and Mrs. Fieldtag, you have a parent-teacher conference after school."

I hate when they do that, Calvin thought as he looked at the twenty four high school students, mostly freshmen, who were shutting down their computers and getting their bags off the ground and from their desks as they lined up at the rear exit to escape to the hallways.

"Please make sure you get your study guides, you will need them as I will not be seeing you again until next Wednesday." Calvin implored to his fourth period Digital Communications class. He knew before the words left his lips that half of the students not only ignored his command, but they wouldn't even study for the state VoCATS exam.

As the bell rang, playing "Forever" by Chris Brown, Calvin watched as all the students exited the door and into the halls, joining the other twenty-one hundred excited students that were happy that not only the school day was coming to an end, but the school year would be over within a week.

Calvin walked to the SMART Board and made sure that it was turned off and then to the projector to make sure that it was turned off and unplugged. He looked down at his crème colored Stafford slacks and his crimson polo with the school's logo on it, making sure he was fresh and clean for the impromptu parent-teacher conference that he knew nothing about. He reached into his black and red Jansport backpack that was at the end of his desk and pulled out a brush and a mirror so that he could make sure his hair was on point, brushing his sharp goatee and checking to make sure his face didn't look drained from dealing with smart mouth and disrespectful students all day.

"What's with the parent-teacher conference?" Miguel Santana, his mentor teacher who taught Auto Body and Mechanics inquired as he stepped into the classroom. Calvin looked down at the olive-colored man who was almost seven inches shorter than his six foot frame and whose work uniform hung loosely on his frail body.

"I have no idea." Calvin replied as he returned the grooming items to his bag. "I don't remember being called to a parent-teacher conference."

"Must be code for some bull crap." Miguel responded frustratingly while shaking his head. "Usually, at the end of the school year, the administration calls various teachers down to the office to let them know that they are letting them go or transferring them—that could be what it is."

Calvin didn't hide look of disappointment on his face. He tried to evaluate his performance during the year and couldn't remember any discipline actions that would have warranted his release one way or the other.

"Don't sweat it, tell me about it when the meeting is over." Miguel tried to encourage him. "We'll try to end our mentor meeting early so that you can get out of here and get to Winston-Salem on time for your night class."

"Thanks." Calvin responded as Miguel left. Calvin looked at his mini bookshelf and reached for his worn and tattered New Revised Standard Version bible and quickly found the worlds to Psalm 91. The inspirational and strengthening psalm calmed his spirit and he knew that no matter what happened that God had his back no matter what.

Calvin was pleased that all the students had followed his directions and turned off their computers. As he got ready to go to this "meeting," he grabbed his backpack and threw it over his shoulder. He stepped out of his classroom and looked down hall and noted the long walk he would have from his room to the administrative office.

He heard some of the students talking about parties and who was dating who and other gossip as he made his way to the office. He responded in kind to a couple of the students who saw him in passing. Once he finally made it to the lobby area next to the cafeteria, he saw Dr. Heath Hewett talking with some of the other younger teachers doing hall duty. Dr. Hewett was relatively young, rumored to be closer to thirty-five. His wild, mop style hair cut was inspired by Ashton Kutcher, yet, he bore a striking resemblance to the Brad Pitt that starred in *Thelma & Louise*. Calvin took a quick look before him at the man who was a mere three inches shorter than he. Upon making eye contact, he saw Dr. Hewett lifting up his walkie talkie and saying something.

"Mr. Rice, follow me," he commanded as if he were leading Calvin to the detention center instead of his office. Calvin walked into the main office and saw some of the student volunteers on the phone and some of the teachers going for their mailboxes as they too were rushing out of school to get a head start on their weekend. He looked at the brightly colored peacock that reminded him of the NBC logo that stood proud on its base as the school mascot. Calvin followed Dr. Hewett through the small teacher work area and down the white and light green hallway to the end of hall. Traces of ginger, wild rose, clover and lavender assaulted Calvin's nose as the aromas escaped the opened door to Dr. Hewett's office.

It had been Calvin's first trip to the principal's office since he started his position as a career and technical education teacher at Butler J. Parker High School in Concord, North Carolina. As he followed the young principal who was walking to a chair in the conference area of his office, he couldn't believe the number of trophies, plaques and memorabilia from Garner-Webb University that packed his large, basketball court-sized office.

As Calvin sat down at the conference table, he was amazed at the number of pictures Dr. Hewett had on his ebony bookshelf. Dr. Hewett's lovely wife reminded him of the R & B singer, Gina Thompson of "The Things You Do" fame. Pictures of their two boys playing baseball and soccer were placed on either side of the larger, prominent picture of a younger Dr. Hewett holding a trophy with his high school soccer team. On his desk, Calvin found the Caribbean Ginger Soy Candle by Soul Purpose, the source of the fragrance in the room.

"That is a captivating and calming smell," the voice of Wes Johnson, the Assistant Principal of Instruction and Calvin's immediate supervisor brought him to his direction. Calvin hadn't even known that the former wide receiver for the Philadelphia Eagles was in his presence. Surprisingly, Wes was wearing a polo shirt with the initials of the black college he and Calvin both attended during their undergrad years over his heart. "I see that my wife has gotten to you too."

"And me," Calvin noticed the other older assistant principal, Evelyn Carter, the sandy blonde older tan-colored lady sat next to Wes. With her short plump frame and aging features, she fit right in with one of the ladies from *The Golden Girls.* "The Happy Feet Collection and the Herbal Spa Wrap are my favorite."

All this talk about Soul Purpose made him wonder what his wife, Maria was doing now. When he brought her to Butler J. Parker High shortly after getting his teaching position earlier this school year, Sheila Johnson, Wes's wife, wasted no time helping Maria become an independent consultant and now, she was selling products and traveling across the state selling products and trying to build her own team.

"Calvin, we brought you here to talk about your evaluation and your progress as a teacher here at Butler J. Parker High School and the Cabarrus County School district." Dr. Hewett started the conversation as he handed a stack of papers and folders that had his name on it and some of the notes and documentations from the evaluations from the three principals as well as from his graduate professor at North Carolina A&T State University. He was familiar with these documents as he'd gone over them with both Miguel and Wes during their new teacher meetings.

Even though Calvin was slightly nervous, he was determined not to show it. He thought about what Miguel had said earlier and he had decided that either destination was not good. He was in the middle of his Master's of Art in Teaching program at A&T and he didn't want to lose his teaching job and not be able to finish the program. This was his first year teaching at a high school as well as being in graduate school for business education and he wanted to succeed in both and do well. He had just finished his student teaching assignment with the school earlier the semester and he was nine hours away from clearing his lateral entry teaching license and turning it into a regular one.

Calvin looked at the documents. He received standard or above standard performance evaluation in almost every facet his observation. His only below standard was on management of student behavior. He knew that was because he didn't address a smart comment made at the beginning of one of the observations, instead, preferring to deal with the student after class. Other than that, everything else was on point or at least that's what he thought.

"We have decided to place you on an action plan." Dr. Hewett continued to as he passed another set of documents for Calvin to look at. "Basically, what we do with this program is that we help all teachers work on different teaching techniques and strategies so that we can help them become better educators. Think of it as an opportunity to strengthen your weaknesses."

Calvin nodded his head, taking in the information. He knew that he wasn't the best teacher in the world, but he was striving to become better. "What does the program entail? And will it interfere with my graduate studies?"

"Oh no," Wes spoke up. "We pair you with senior teachers who will evaluate your techniques and offer constructive criticism to help you become a better teacher. All first year teachers go through the program on a local level and we find that many of them come out to become better teachers. This won't interfere with grad school at all and we want you to succeed in that too so that you can clear your license."

Calvin read over the papers and didn't see anything that indicated that his head was on the chopping block.

The way Dr. Hewett and Wes were talking, they wanted him to stay. "Sounds like a plan." Calvin gave his first response after looking up from the documents. "Anything that will help me become a better teacher is what I want and I'm willing to do that."

"Yeah…" Evelyn jumped in and paused, "there's nothing wrong with being on an action plan. Look at is as a positive thing that will enhance your teaching experience."

"We need you to sign these papers saying that we explained to you about the program and your willingness to participate. And we'll set everything up when you come back and join us next year."

Calvin shook each of the administrators' hands and he grabbed the papers and put them in the backpack and got up to leave. He looked at his watch and realized he barely had two hours to get from Concord to his class in Greensboro which was an hour and a half away and with it being a Friday night, he knew that he would need each minute in order to make sure he got to the class on time.

"Everything okay bruh?" He heard Wes catching up with him. Calvin had looked up to Wes. He valued their time together as they reviewed his evaluations and presentations during the graduate school. On a personal level sharing many things in common, including a brotherhood.

"I'm good. For a minute there, I thought y'all were going to try to take my job."

"Bruh, now you know I'm not gonna let them do that. We need more of us in the schools if you know what I mean."

Calvin did know what he meant. For a whole year and a half while working at a middle school in Winston-Salem, he'd heard advertisements on the radio and saw the billboards advertising the need for more black male teachers. After being a substitute teacher and a long-term assistant teacher and receiving rave reviews from his fellow teachers and administrators alike, Calvin made the jump from assistant teacher and accepted the offer at Butler J. Parker. He felt he had answered his calling.

"Yeah, it's good to see more black men—Godly men, in the schools. Help save a generation."

Calvin and Wes did a one handed grip and then they parted ways. Calvin rushed to his class and grabbed a few books so he could head out.

"How did the meeting go?" Miguel had changed into a school T-shirt and was void of any oil on his hands.

"Pretty good. They were telling me about an action plan program that sounded exciting and would help me improve to be a better teacher."

"Oh okay. Exciting huh?"

"Yeah have you heard of it?"

"Nope, it's new to me. I've never heard of it."

"As soon as I get some more information on it, I'll pass it on to you. I'm going to go ahead and go to Greensboro so I don't be late to class."

"Alright man, I'll talk to you Monday. And you be careful on the drive back to Greensboro and to Winston-Salem...I don't see how you do it."

"God makes a way."

"Yes he does."

***

The Rice Residence
Winston-Salem, North Carolina
10:25 PM

After sitting in his teaching reading class for three hours, Calvin was exhausted. He looked at the wedding band on his left hand. His thoughts went to Maria and he couldn't wait to see her. He'd surprised her by getting her favorite Japanese takeout, hibachi chicken with mixed vegetables, sweet carrots and ginger sauce with iced tea. For himself, he stuck with the teriyaki chicken, sweet carrots and steamed rice.

Calvin opened the door and he was surprised to hear Luther Vandross blasting from the stereo that was in their room. As he walked in and took off his shoes near the door, he noticed a nice pair of black Kenneth Cole dress shoes next to his wife's stilettos.

I don't wear Kenneth Cole, Calvin thought to himself as he quickly slid out of his shoes and walked to place the food on the table. He turned on the light and he could see two plates and smell the seafood in the air. Upon closer inspection, he could smell the vanilla candle struggling to make its identity known and saw the empty Red Lobster bags that were in the trash.

Calvin made a turn to the hallway that led to their master bedroom and he opened the door to his room. Calvin's eyes got as big as saucers as he saw Maria in bed with Deacon Bilal Kodjoe of Cleveland Missionary Baptist Church. He knew Deacon Kodjoe because his ministry group often partnered with to do faith-based and service initiative projects with the young men in his church. Calvin saw the naked man doing things with his wife that only he should've been entitled to. Feeling violated in a major way, he stormed his marriage bed. Calvin attacked the well-built man and forgot for a few moments he was Christian. The carnal rage took over.

Chapter Ten

Wednesday, August 20, 2008
Butler J. Parker High School
2:25 PM

Calvin didn't kill Bilal. The thought crossed his mind—he definitely had the advantage. But Calvin wasn't the man of Christ he had proclaimed to be as he beat Bilal like he stole something—and technically he did—he had stolen his night of passion to be with his wife. After the drive from school to his graduate class and then the little trip made Calvin in and throughout Winston-Salem until he had reached his condo near the corner of Silas Creek Parkway and University Parkway, which was about a mile north of Wake Forest University, Calvin had expected to have a romantic dinner with his wife and then the right to consummate his marriage in a manner approved by God.

Rahliem arrived at the condo ten minutes before the police did. Maria had called him after she called the police in hopes that his friend would talk some sense into him. Rahliem was able to pull Calvin off of the man and keep him restrained while Bilal made his great escape. After the police arrived, Rahliem dealt with the cops and by the grace of God, kept them from filing charges against Calvin after agreeing to have Calvin vacate the condo and enroll in an anger management class.

Calvin had spent most of the summer at Rahliem's apartment in the south side of Winston-Salem near Hanes Mall. Rahliem had just married and had a few months left on the lease to his apartment. Calvin was stressed. Dealing with the fact that Maria was bold enough to have an affair with someone they both knew and respected was too much. Calvin dropped out of summer school and withdrew from the second session. This move delayed his graduation plans a semester. While at Rahliem's, Calvin went to the anger management classes and also worked a second job as a waiter at a popular upscale vegetarian restaurant near downtown. He'd also temporarily gotten Maria to see a marriage counselor so that he could save his marriage, but after five sessions, Maria stopped attending.

Two weeks prior to this moment, Calvin had moved back into his home and marriage seemed to be agreeing with the two of them. Calvin and Maria openly talked about their failure to start the family they had always wanted. They had discussed how the two failed pregnancies seemed to be the underlying rift in their marriage. They wanted to try again at conception. Maria had finally gotten another job. No wait, Maria's foster mother was able to pull some strings and get Maria her job back as a teller for Bank of America. Maria benefited from having a new customer base to sell her Soul Purpose products and build her business. Calvin began to use more of the organic products and he liked how the products made him feel. They also served other purposes they served when he and Maria would spend quality time doing their thing in the bedroom. In an effort to attempt a couple activity that was recommended by the counselors, Calvin also joined Soul Purpose as an independent consult and worked with Maria as they hosted house parties on Saturdays after they had worked their respective jobs throughout the week.

Calvin had a week to get ready before students came back to school. This would be his second semester as a teacher. It took some strings being pulled and some favors being performed for him to get this job as an educator. His confession to murdering a fourteen year old boy when he was twelve came up and his brother was still serving time for his crime. Plus Calvin had the sales and marketing experience and given his background, he didn't think working with a group of troubled teens in a low performing school would be too much of a stretch. Calvin saw this as an opportunity to demonstrate his love for Jesus Christ and save a few souls while teaching important job skills that most employers now required of their new hires.

Calvin had looked forward to the beginning of the school year. He anticipated the new challenges the new school year would bring. Two years ago, Calvin started a job as a teacher's assistant at a middle school in High Point. This was a welcomed changed from the sales and business environment he'd been accustomed to.

Calvin's initial assignment was to help English Language Learners who could not read in their own language and were struggling to read and learn in English. With the seventh and eighth graders, he worked with Ms. Salazar, the English as a Second Language teacher who did classroom activities. Calvin and Ms. Salazar, also went over the student's assignments they received in their English, social studies and science classes to make sure they understood what the assignment was asking for and that they could do the assignment. It was when he worked with the sixth graders that Calvin got a chance to shine. The teacher would work with most of the class while Calvin spent most of his time with the six students in two classes who did not know how to read. In some ways, Calvin had his own classroom because he had access to Hooked on Phonics and worked with flash cards and had an audio tape. As the assistant teacher, Calvin spent on average thirty minutes a day each school day with two sixth grade students. They worked through story books that were eight to twelve pages, work sheets and other gadgets that helped measured their progression in reading.

Calvin always saw himself teaching. With his undergraduate degree being in business, his choices were to obtain a second undergraduate degree or to move into the Master's program. With the time spent in each program equaling to about three years, he thought that the Master's degree would be worth more so he entered A&T's program so he could build on the knowledge he already had in the business field. After having passed both Praxis tests prior to entering a teaching program, Calvin had already demonstrated an ability to be able to do the class work.

Those moves, as well as a glowing recommendation from the administration at the middle school led to Calvin being able to accept a teaching assignment at Butler J. Parker High School in Concord, North Carolina.

The rules and the assignment would be different.

No working with Mrs. Salazar to make sure students were getting the undivided attention they needed. No more lunch breaks with the other vocational teacher's where they could strategize and offer tips and solutions to dealing with students who were a bit "troubling." Calvin graduated and walked into his very own classroom. And for his first semester, despite a few blemishes, Calvin thought he was okay.

Butler J. Parker was in south Concord near Concord Mills and the Lowes Motor Speedway near North Charlotte off of I-85. The school was so close to Charlotte, one could spit and it would land in the city. Riding through the trees and the shade would have a newcomer thinking they were in the middle of the woods and that would be hunting for an old cabin.

About a quarter of a mile into the woods, the school made itself visible. It's a two level, red and white brick building that was the length of three football fields. The teacher's parking lot was to the right of the school and the school's football field was to the left. To the right of the entryway to the school were three flagpoles; one for our country's flag, one for the state flag and one for the school flag. Once Calvin got out of the car and left the car in the parking lot, Calvin would walk on the sidewalk that was decorated in red and peach bricks, giving the illusion of the yellow brick road like the one in *The Wizard of Oz.*

When Calvin walked into the school, he walked past the gymnasium and could see some of the students running laps in the indoor track on the right. To the left was the school office, where he goes to his mailbox and get the mail for the day. The faculty and staff had returned to school on Monday to attend mandatory meetings and trainings to prepare for the new school year. When Calvin pulled his mail from the box that had Mr. Rice written in script, he seen that he had papers filed with the ABC's. In education, there were so many different forms and paperwork to have to fill out as it relates to different student's disabilities and other issues until no one calls the form by its name; the forms are often referred to by its three to five letter abbreviation.

The first form Calvin looked at as he headed to his classroom was an IEP, or an individual education plan. The purpose of this form was to notify him about the goals and objectives of a student's education plan and modifications needed to help the student be successful in a given class. The BMPs were behavior modification plans that dictated the level of interventions and disciplines the students needed. Calvin heard of these documents when he was in the middle school he worked at last year but this would be the first time he would have access to them.

In North Carolina, they had gotten rid of the keyboarding class that many of his classmates in high school went through to teach students how to use the computer. Instead, they replaced that class with the class he was teaching called Digital Communications which was designed to teach about basic computer concepts. Digital Communications was *supposed* to be a class that only dealt with students who had failed the Computer Competency Test that was given to eighth graders during the fall.

What ended up happening was that in addition to the students who failed the test, guidance counselors and others used the class as a "float" class for students who couldn't take any more classes, or for seniors who were about to graduate who needed an "easy" class credit.

Everyone and their mama was put in the class regardless of individual need or even desire to be in the class. Because of this, Calvin really had his heart set on teaching the Business Law or Accounting classes because he enjoyed teaching those subjects. He got a chance to observe when he worked on his field study the previous fall and he knew when he accepted the position at Butler J. Parker, the teacher who had been teaching those courses had retired. Calvin was under the impression that those classes would be the ones he would be teaching because in his job interview, those were the main classes that were discussed as being part of his teaching duties. He had been assured all through the last semester that his efforts to market the Accounting and Business Law classes had led to enough students enrolling in the courses and that he'd be rewarded for his efforts by teaching his desired classes.

"Thank you for agreeing to change schedules with me. Those Digital Communications classes are a mess." Calvin looked up and over to his right and realized that Bonnie Clayborne was speaking to him. The older white lady was in her sixties and Calvin could smell the cigarettes she had been smoking, before he could see her. Calvin, as well as most of the students and faculty were so used to smelling the cigarettes on her that they took the tart smoky smell to be part of her natural aroma. Calvin remembered the last year when he did a tour of the school, he could hear her screaming and shouting at her kids and he thought to himself how happy he was not to have her teaching assignment.

Calvin was heated because he didn't agree to change schedules with anyone. Calvin didn't want to assume that this was her doing…at least not yet.

"Today is the first day I found out that I would be teaching Digital Communications."

"Really?" As Bonnie got excited, he could see the wrinkles in her face move and slowly show the surprised emotion on her face. "Dr. Hewett said that he spoke with you over the summer and you would be okay with the schedule change."

That's a lie, Calvin thought to himself. He spent most of the summer dealing with his wife's infidelity, attempting to rebuild their marriage and trying to keep his mind preoccupied so he wouldn't be tempted to kill Bilal. What Dr. Hewett probably meant to say was that he *meant* to get in touch with him, *meant* to ask him if it was okay to change classes. But the truth of the matter was Calvin was employed at the school, not running his own business. That meant that the principal and the powers that be could make the decision to change his schedule. If he wanted to keep his job, he would have to go along with it. Truth be told, Calvin was mad at Dr. Hewett for changing the schedule and assuming that he would be okay with it. Digital Communications was his least favorite of all of the Business Education classes being taught in the high schools. When he was a high school student, he had taken a lot of the business courses as preparation for his undergraduate degree that he earned at Winston-Salem State.

"If I were you I'd be mad," Bonnie went on, seeming to get excited about the possibility of stirring up some trouble between Calvin and Dr. Hewett. Calvin noted by the look on her face that she'd get her jollies off if she could get him into some trouble. "Dr. Hewett is always being sneaky, conniving and nasty. It's possible that another one of the teachers will switch schedules with you, but with the student schedules already being printed up and ready for distribution at the open house tonight."

As Calvin looked at his new teaching schedule, he could smell that old Sapphire by Elizabeth Taylor perfume whiff through the air. He knew that meant that Evelyn was nearby. This semester, he was scheduled to teach three units of Digital Communications.

Planning from 7:30 AM to 9:00 AM.
2nd Period is from 9:07 AM to 10:43 AM
3rd Period is from 10:50 AM to 1:00 PM
Lunch is from 11:54 AM to 12:21PM
4th Period is from 1:00 PM to 2:30 PM

Calvin shook his head at the news because the only thing worse than having to teach three classes of a subject he hated most was to have the planning period first thing in the morning after morning duty. Calvin would've liked to have had planning second or third after warming up with a 1st Period class. With a first period planning period, he still had to clock in by 6:30 am, which Dr. Hewett required of the teachers at Butler J. Parker. At least once and sometimes twice a week, Calvin would have to give up his first period planning to attend an IEP meeting for an EC student in the exceptional children's department. The meetings were mandatory because they dealt with the student's mental disability and the plan for meeting the need for their education. The parents often were only able to come during first period before they went off to work. Calvin didn't mind going to the meetings because he saw himself as having an opportunity to be a good steward and part of the solution to making the student's learning environment better.

First period planning was often a popular time for "mandatory" training sessions and other meetings that seemed to take place between county administrators and faculty. This meant the only time he would have to actually plan would be the twenty six minutes he had for lunch when the students left and the extra hour or two he stayed after school after the last bell rung.

Once Calvin stepped foot into the classroom, he could hear someone calling his name on the intercom.

"Mr. Rice, are you in?" Ms. Cooper, the receptionist up front had cut into his line. Immediately, he panicked because the last time someone called him on the intercom at work, was at the middle school when he learned that his son, Carlton, II. had died at the hospital and he had to take off work to get to the emergency room.

"Yes ma'am, I just walked in."

"Oh good, your mother is on line two and I'm going to put her on the phone okay."

"No, problem, thank you." Calvin played it cool but in reality, he was disturbed as to why his mother would be calling him at work. She was two time zones and a mountain away and rarely did she call him at work when she always sent him a text message to his phone. "Hello?" Calvin was frantic and anticipated the bad news she might bring.

"Oh darling calm down, it's just me," his mother-in-law was acting all bougie on the phone. Mrs. Vargas became Maria's foster mother once Maria made her way from El, Paso to Denver, Colorado. Calvin took the receiver away from his ear and looked at it. He was tempted to hang up the phone. She got on his *last* nerves with that mess. Calvin could feel his heart beating fast and he tried to quell his anger so that he wouldn't curse the woman who raised his wife, out. He shook his head because this was just one more stunt that Mrs. Vargas was known for. He could imagine her sitting behind her desk, leaning back in her chair and just tossing her hair around just so she could feel it bounce. Having just arrived from Mexico three years ago, she'd already adopted black culture as her own, tailoring her new accent, speech patterns and her mannerisms after the women of *Girlfriends, Soul Food* and *The Parkers*. It was hard to believe that she wasn't coming to America.

Satisfied that everything was normal, Calvin inquired, "Everything fine at home?"

"Yes, I just wanted to speak with you at work, that's all."

"Mrs. Vargas."

Before Calvin could finish speaking his mother-in-law cut him off, "Calvin Rice, I *know* you don't have the gall to be formal with me!"

"No disrespect *mother* but I am at work, you know I cannot be on the phone with personal business. I just stepped foot in the classroom and I need to set up for our open house and be ready to meet my student's parents." Calvin wanted this annoying woman off his line and he wanted her off his line.

Calvin should have just hung up the phone and then claimed that the call got lost. Last time he tried that Claudia Vargas came to the school, demanded to see him and then cursed him out for twenty four minutes and fifteen seconds of *his* lunch break—the other forty five seconds he got to breathe. Calvin had no choice but to be diplomatic with her.

"Well hijo, I want not for much, just to say hello is all." She's supposed to be the branch manager of the bank service center in the predominant Hispanic area of Winston-Salem but instead she was the branch manager of getting on his nerves.

"Madre, I got to go. The principal just walked in," Calvin tried to rush her off the phone. He had a lot of work to do before he met some of the students and their parents and he wasn't going to let the mother-in-law ruin his ability to get in his way.

"Well you tell that sexy Brad Pitt-wanna be I said hello. Chao!"

Mrs. Vargas was so fake Calvin wished he could slap some realness into her. The fact that she was six foot in heels probably wouldn't stop him except he thought about his wife. He'd never hit her no matter how mad she made him so slapping her mother just wouldn't seem right. The thought had crossed his mind when he was beating Bilal to a pulp but he knew he couldn't do it.

Calvin looked up from his desk and spoke of the devil too soon. He didn't see Dr. Hewett walking into the classroom. The man was turning on one of the computers and logging in to play Mahjong Titans. Upon closer inspection, he realized that Mrs. Vargas was right about Dr. Hewett, he does look a little like Brad Pitt, even with him slouching in the seat a little. The Unforgettable fragrance Dr. Hewett was wearing made Calvin remember that in addition to being his boss, he's a *huge* P. Diddy fan. That man worshiped the ground Sean Combs walked on. When Calvin met Dr. Hewett for his interview, he was surprised to see a big replica of the Bad Boy Entertainment logo on the way. On his desk was a copy of the gold plaque that was earned for the work done one of their albums.

Calvin stood up from his very comfortable black chair while Dr. Hewett approached him.

"I heard you were talking to Ms. Clayborne about your new schedule. Is there a problem with it?" Dr. Hewett asked the question he should have known the answer to. He took his ear piece off which made Calvin wonder whether or not he heard him tell his mother-in-law to get off the phone. Then he remembered that he wasn't at the call center he used to work at any more so he could breathe a little bit.

"I didn't anticipate having to change my schedule and lesson plans from the Business Law and Computerized Accounting classes I thought I would be teaching."

"Well *I* have to make decisions that are in the best interest of our school and our students. I hope you understand that."

"That I do." What was Calvin going to say? The students had already been told to expect him as their teacher and he was still relatively new and he didn't have any seniority and didn't have anywhere to go that would sustain him and Maria comfortably if he were to lose this job over his refusal to accept his new teaching assignment.

"I realize that you just lost your second child about a year or so ago." Calvin couldn't believe the gall Dr. Hewett had in bringing up a sensitive and personal matter into their conversation. Dr. Hewett didn't *know* him well enough to have that conversation with him. He made a note to have a conversation with Wes about him telling Dr. Hewett his personal business. Wes was the only one at the school besides Miguel who knew about the loss of the child. "So you don't have the toddler or a newborn sitting at home depending on you so you can buy them diapers and clothes and other necessities they need. Even if you did, I figured that with your being young and newly married that you could handle some students who may get out of line every now and then. Ms. Clayborne is on her way out of here. I can't get rid of her just yet because she is going to transfer to the new school once it opens next school year. It's not her fault or mine that the school was not ready to be opened this school year as scheduled."

"I understand," Calvin replied humbly.

"Besides, I figure that this would be a better position for you than working at McDonalds."

"Excuse me," Calvin was shocked that Dr. Hewett would disrespect him like that.

"Understand something Calvin. Just as fast I as brought you to this school I can arrange for your dismissal. I'm sure there are others who would be happy to be in the position you are in. Now if you have any more complaints about what I do and how I run this school, I'd appreciate it if you'd say it to my face and not behind my back or in the staff mail room where everyone can hear you."

Dr. Hewett was showing how evil he could be. Calvin had been warned before he accepted the assignment from some of the former teachers as well as some of the current ones that Dr. Hewett's new attitude came courtesy of Donald Trump. Ever since *The Apprentice*, it seemed like supervisors everywhere grew nuts the size of grapefruits and were testing their powers on earth with anyone who they think doesn't have the power or wherewithal to defend themselves.

"Oh, and your mother—tell the chick not to make personal calls while you on the clock. She's supposed to be running things at Bank of America. If she feels that she needs to be that controlling, then you need to join her over there. I'm sure they can use someone of your talents there."

"Wait a minute Dr. Hewett, I think you are out of line here." Calvin could not believe this bastard had the gall to come at his mother-in-law like that. It's one thing when he did it but Dr. Hewett didn't know her like that. Calvin looked at Dr. Hewett and all of a sudden he didn't look like Brad Pitt. He clicked the ear piece, told the caller that he would return their call and then he turned it off.

"No Calvin, I'm never out of line. If your mother doesn't stop calling you for non-emergency issues, you will be without a job. I don't do socializing and playing around on the taxpayer's clock and I don't expect any of the teachers who work here to participate in the same."

That was the icing on the cake. Calvin was fuming mad when Dr. Hewett walked toward the door, spoke into the phone and resumed the call he had returned. The Unforgettable fragrance was lingering in the air from the space they shared. Now he was forced to smell him while trying to get some work done for the next hour or so. It couldn't get any worse than this.

Calvin began to understand why a job like this could be stressful at times. Not only was he under pressure to make sure state test scores went up and to educate and motivate students to learn; he had to put up with arrogant jerks like Dr. Hewett. He remembered last year when he first came to this school and thought that this would be a great place to work.

He wished he wasn't driving sixty five miles every day from Winston-Salem to Concord. Calvin began to think he should have just stayed where he was at. He figured Dr. Hewett was going to be the root to a lot of his problems and tested how saved he *really* was.

For a moment, Calvin entertained Satan's suggestion. A flashback of when a twelve year old Calvin pulled the trigger and murdered someone entered his mind. Garfield, the gang member and bully from his childhood, fell hard on the grass. Calvin replaced Garfield's face with Dr. Hewett.

I rebuke you in the name of Jesus, he said to himself. He didn't want the monster within him to return. The best way to avoid that was to keep a safe distance between Dr. Hewett and himself.

Chapter Eleven

Friday, August 22, 2008
Butler J. Parker High School
12:25 PM

"I can't believe Heath did that to you," Miguel was angered after Calvin relayed the whole incident to him. He hadn't had a chance to talk to Miguel on Wednesday or Thursday.

They decided for his teacher mentorship that they would have lunch after school at a local Japanese restaurant. After retelling his story, Calvin was no longer interested in hearing about Dr. Hewett or the school he worked for. "He can be a jerk sometimes. But no matter what, don't let that man or none of the other two-faced people in that administration make you quit."

Calvin nodded his head. "Never that. I invested too much money and time into pursuing this education degree for me to walk away now." After taking a few bites of his food, he continued, "I can't wait for this action plan program to get started so I can meet with some other teachers who may have some insight on my situation. I remember Wes saying that they had hired a new marketing teacher that used to teach some of the business classes and I can see that working in my favor."

"I agree. And plus you know I'm still here—even though I do more with auto body and future mechanics," Miguel encouraged.

"Many of those future mechanics begin thinking about owning their own shop or at least they manage one," Calvin pointed out.

"And a few of them take your class."

Calvin noted and continued eating his food. His phone rang and he saw Maria's name on the caller ID. He took out his LG flip phone and answered the call. "Hey Baby, how are you?"

"Hey sweetie," she sounded so sexy. He was almost embarrassed to be sitting across from Miguel in public, blushing. "I'm good, I'm good. Can you stop by Papa John's on your way home? Send me a text when you leave and I'll order the pizza about thirty minutes afterwards so that by time you get to Winston and to the store, it can be ready."

Calvin thought about the extra sit-ups and laps he was going to have to run in order to lose the calories that the pizza was sure to stack on top of the Japanese food he was eating. He looked at his nearly finished plate of teriyaki chicken and mixed vegetables and he figured that he could maybe pass if he only had two slices of pizza and drank water.

"No problem. I'm in a meeting with Miguel and I'll see you when I get home."

"Alright."

After hearing the dial tone, Calvin hung up the phone.

"Can I keep it real with you for a minute?" Miguel asked once Calvin put the phone on the table.

"Aw come on, you always keep it real," Calvin responded.

"Wes is not who you think he is," Miguel packed up his food in the "to-go" box he had the waiter bring when he brought their meal.

"Why you say that?"

If there was a thorn in their mentor/mentee relationship, it was the fact that it was known that Miguel and Wes hardly ever got along. The dislike was so bad that even the students knew about it. The students placed bets on who they thought would win and openly made jokes about an upcoming fight between the two in the student foyer. The phone rang again and at the sight of his mother-in-law's phone number through the screen, Calvin wanted to hurl the little phone clear across the restaurant.

"I'm just saying, have you walked into his office lately?" Miguel inquired.

Calvin recalled the crimson carpet and the large wooden crest of their fraternity's shield that hung on the right side of the wall. The white lamps and decorations he had were replaced with Indian and Middle Eastern statues and portraits depicting a man sitting "lotus position" as if he were chanting. He felt that Wes's tastes were eclectic and thought nothing about his taste in décor. "Doesn't it bother your spirit a little bit?"

Calvin thought about it and had to admit that he found Wes's new found interest in Indian culture slightly weird. It reminded him of a few scenes in the movie *What's Love Got to Do With It* but he knew that Wes didn't like Tina Turner like that. Wes used to bash her on a regular when they were in undergrad.

"I'm not a fan of the way his office is now, but that's just his office. I don't see how a change in a couple of designs would affect the man's attitude or how he feels about me."

"Calvin, let me break it down for you. Wes is a Buddhist and probably has been one for many years. When he was the CTE Coordinator, he could be heard chanting and humming. I hated walking past his office…"

"Wes is not a Buddhist." Calvin cut Miguel off. "We used to pray together and go to church and all that. He used to stay on me about reading my Bible and everything else."

"I can't make you change your mind if you don't believe it. I don't know what to say. I know you and him have a bond and I'm not trying to come between that. What I am trying to do is to warn you if nothing else that you need to view Heath, Evelyn and Wes on the same level. Don't think that because you and him are 'brothers' that you are going to have special privileges. He's going to throw you under the bus the minute he gets the chance."

To avoid a confrontation after a nice meal, Calvin just shook his head. One of the things that he loved about Miguel was that Miguel had always shown himself to be a Man of God. Miguel had invited him to a meeting with a few teachers who worked with the Fellowship of Christian Athletes chapter at Butler J. Parker. The teachers not only prayed with the athletes before games and tryouts but also found comfort in being able to have short Bible Studies when they ended up staying late. A few times, the teachers prayed for safe passage for him as he made the trek from Concord to Winston-Salem, asking God for traveling grace and mercy.

"I don't want you to leave here mad at me."

"I'm not mad." Calvin replied quickly. Even though he didn't cut the man off, he realized that his actions could've been interpreted as rude. "I'm sorry man. I know you are just trying to help me and I really appreciate all that you are doing for me. I just know that I've known Wes longer than you and I think if he were Buddhist, he'd tell me."

The waiter came and offered the men two separate bills. Each of them pulled out credit cards. "I got this one," Miguel reached for the Calvin's bill. "You pay for the next one."

"Are you sure?"

"I wouldn't have offered if I wasn't. Besides, I know that you and Maria have something planned for the night. Go ahead and surprise her with some roses or something special—perhaps intimate."

Calvin chuckled at the thought of the older man encouraging him to make love to his wife.

"I'm glad that the two of you are working things out," Miguel encouraged as they got up to get ready to go.

"Yeah, the counseling is helping and things are getting better in other areas. We even talked about the possibility of trying to have another child."

"Sounds like you have your night planned. If you ever decide you want to a child to practice with, I've got five of them for you borrow for a couple of days."

"Naw man. When that time comes for us to be parents again, I'm sure we'll have our hands full."

The waiter was expeditious in bringing Miguel the check back. Calvin reached in his pocket and pulled out a five bill and stuffed it in the gracious waiter's hands.

"Thank you," be heard the mild mannered gentleman who could've passed as a student in his class reply.

"No problem."

As they walked out of the restaurant, Miguel followed Calvin to his car. "Before you leave, let us say a quick prayer for the road."

"Thanks."

Calvin and Miguel bowed their heads and Miguel spoke up in prayer. "Our Father God, the Great Jehovah, We thank you for allowing us to have another satisfying meal and for all that you have done for us this day. Please forgive us of any transgressions that may have knowingly or unknowingly entered our minds and settled in our spirits. We thank you for what you did on the cross and we ask for traveling mercy as we leave here for our intended destinations. With all good things we give honor and thanks. In your precious son Jesus Christ's name we pray, Amen."

"Amen," Calvin gave the man a hug and watched him get into his brown colored 1990 Mercury Cougar. He got into his white 2006 Ford Focus and started the ignition. He saw the gas meter was low and knew he'd be spending another fifty dollars on gas before he got home. At times he wished he was able to get one of the teaching jobs he had applied for with Winston-Salem/ Forsyth County Schools or neighboring Guilford County Schools, which covered Greensboro and High Point, but he had been unsuccessful. A few of the interviews he had gone on had not yielded positive results and thus he was in Concord for another year. Next year, he would seriously consider transferring or even going back to substituting but for the moment he was content with having a job and decided to stick it out for now. The year couldn't get any worse. He pulled out his phone and sent Maria a quick text message letting her know that he was on his way home.

***

Mrs. Vargas continued to blow up his phone and Calvin had spent the better part of the ride on I-85 North and US 52 ignoring her. She caused enough inconvenience in his life for a week and Calvin didn't want to be bothered. Once he had gotten to Welcome, North Carolina, he got in the right lane, lowered the speed on his car from seventy to sixty miles per hour and put the car on cruise control. He returned her phone call, knowing that in about five minutes or less, Sprint was going to drop his call because of the lack of service in the area.

"You're ignoring your mother today, what's wrong?"

Calvin strongly disliked the idea that his mother-in-law preferred that Calvin refer to her as "mother" or "mama." For one, Calvin didn't feel her like that and two, he felt that she was too much into their business as it was. She was always putting her two cents into their marriage and her ideas on how things should've gone. Never mind the fact that the woman had divorced husband number three a few weeks before Calvin and Maria celebrated their first anniversary, but still…

"I had my teacher-peer meeting today. I'm getting ready for the new school year."

"Oh, that's not important."

If Mrs. Vargas only knew, the teacher peer meetings were required as part of his individual teaching plan and were part of his evaluation. The meetings were definitely important. "I wanted to know what you and Maria's plans were for the weekend. Her foster sisters are coming into town and I think it would be good if y'all took them out to eat or even went to Carowinds or something."

"Maria and I had planned on spending time together, alone. Probably watch a Tyler Perry movie or something."

"*Madea?*" Mrs. Vargas questioned as she were on the stage with her, "that's your problem. How are y'all going to watch a movie about a man dressing as an old woman who claims to have murdered all of her ex-husbands? There's nothing Christian about those movies."

Mrs. Vargas went on and on about how she didn't like Tyler Perry's plays and how he always portrayed the women as battered and a laundry list of other complaints. Just like he knew would happen, as soon as he crossed the Forsyth County line and approached the Hickory Ridge Lane exit, his phone cut off. He chuckled to himself at the thought that Mrs. Vargas would probably spend five more minutes talking until she realized he wasn't on the line anymore. Traffic began to pick up as he approached I-40, he got off on the interstate heading west. Remembering to head to the Papa John's to pick up their pizzas, he remembered Miguel's advice and realized he had enough time to stop at the flower shop off of Peter's Creek Parkway to surprise Maria with a bouquet of her favorite flowers, white roses and pink carnations.

Chapter Twelve

2Pac woke Calvin from his nightmare as he saw death around the corner. The phone had been vibrating all through the night and his wife hadn't heard a peep. He stared at her nude body and thought about his early morning woody that was demanding some attention. As it turned out, they were able to avoid her foster sisters for the weekend and spend more quality time by themselves. Calvin secretly praised Jesus for this miracle even though he knew he would probably repent when he went to church next Sunday. In thirty minutes, Calvin was going to have to get up to get ready for the first day of school. They had just finished making love through the night and Calvin was still hungry for some more. He looked at the clock and noticed a three, a four and a five in consecutive order in bright florescent green lights. Calvin exhaled deeply because in a few more minutes, he would be getting up getting ready to go to school.

The thought had crossed his mind to wake her up for an early morning romp but that phone on the night stand next to her side of the bed just kept on vibrating and getting on his everlasting nerve.

Calvin sat up and looked at the text message:

I'm sorry about the problems I caused between you and your man...but at least he knows now that your heart belongs to me and with me is where you need to be...- Bilal

"Uggh," Calvin growled as he threw the phone against the wall, watched it crack and fall to the floor. Just when he though he and Maria were making progress, he began regretting getting in bed with his cheating Hispanic Kimora Simmons-knock off. He watched her body rise and fall as she snored lightly and his magnificent erection disappeared like a magic trick. Calvin had been working on forgiving Maria for cheating on him. Every time he did, all he could picture was the night that he caught his wife and Bilal around in bed—their marriage bed.

Lately, those moments had become less and less as they struggled to get over the death of their son. He had been the second child they had lost as their first son died as a result of sudden infant death syndrome. Calvin and Maria longed to raise beautiful children, but their failure to deal with their children's deaths were part of their problems.

Having a child had meant the world to them and they'd gone through many lengths to get one. Maria had been through a lot to give them a family; two infant deaths and two miscarriages but they kept trying.

Calvin often wondered if this was the reason that Maria was cheating on him. Wondered if she desired to have a baby by someone else, but he shook the thought aside.

"What's wrong baby?" Maria woke up and started massaging Calvin's back.

"I want to talk about ol' boy."

Maria quickly turned over and huffs, "I'm not going through this again. I said I was sorry."

"Why does he keep calling and texting you?" Calvin gritted through his teeth and then looked at the clock. "It is 3:45 in the morning, can't he respect me enough to call when he thinks I'm at work at least?" Calvin turned over and felt the breeze on his nude body as Maria snatched more of the sheet to cover herself with. "I should have messed him up when I had the chance."

Calvin turned around, met with the frown on her face and turned back on his side of the bed. And just like that, he was seething mad as he watched his wife step into the shower in the bathroom. If only he had the heart to leave her; maybe he could have a shot at being happy with someone else. He noticed that she no longer took pride in going downstairs and fix his breakfast, and he contemplated whether getting a divorce would be the way she was going to get a break, fast. Calvin decided that instead of arguing with his wife about the issue again, he would do best just to go to work early. Going to church and work kept him out of trouble and sometimes, that was the best decision.

Butler J. Parker High School
7:03 AM

Calvin could hear the wheels of his briefcase rolling across the linoleum floor. He walked from the main entrance to the career and technical education hall at the far end of the school. He thought that by leaving early, he could beat the traffic heading into Concord but it was just his luck that there was a major accident on I-85 South right before the first Salisbury exit. Even with three lanes, it took almost thirty minutes to clear that section because a small, silver Honda CRV had been flipped upside down; the right passenger side of a white Nissan Sentra had been smashed in like a crushed soda can into the guard rail. A green Saturn was still in the middle of the lanes. Calvin said a silent prayer for them as he listened to *The Steve Harvey Morning Show*. It was unclear whether or not the driver or any passengers were still in any of the cars, but there were plenty of ambulances, firemen and police officers on the scene trying to get to the victims.

Upon arriving at the school, he had been grateful for another safe journey. He stretched once he got out the car and, realized he had thirty minutes to get ready before the first day of classes began. He was thankful that he was prepared. Once he entered his classroom, he saw a copy of the syllabus, the parental consent forms and the vocabulary sheet his students would use for their first assignment.

Remembering that he had hall monitoring duty at the school entrance, he quickly placed his backpack on the desk and rolled his suitcase under the table where his computer sat. Calvin ran out of the classroom and as he was rounding the corner to head down the hallway, he crashed into a student. The student's iPod exploded on the floor, its shell casing cracked in half and the earphones bounced up and down like tennis balls before making a hard landing on the floor.

"Watch where you're going mother—" a deep voice commanded and Calvin shook his head. He couldn't believe that the student had the gall to call him one of the most profane names in the English language. Calvin got a look at the student's face and he noticed the soft, puppy-like features on the student's face. The puffy cheeks gave the Michelin man a run for his money and the soft, stuffed animal-like frame betrayed the gangster persona the student attempted to intimidate him with. The braided cornrows looked freshly done and the student's scalp smelled of hemp and grape seed oil, but gave the hair a nice shine. The strong and refreshing mix of woods, spices and musk began to infiltrate Calvin's air space, the eyes betrayed the student and revealed her true gender.

"My fault Mr. Rice," the student talked to him and flashed a quick smile, showing straight, white smile. "I thought you were one of the jerks not watching where they were going. Thought I was gonna have to set you straight."

"I'm fine." Calvin shook himself off. He started to address the fact that calling him "mother" anything was beyond inappropriate. Calvin didn't feel like going back to his class or asking another teacher for a discipline referral and he definitely didn't want to send a student to the administrator before the first day of school could officially began.

"I'm Charlie," she reached her hand out to him as if she were on equal footing with him and looked him in the eye. "I'll be in your second period class in about two hours."

"Nice to meet you, I got to get to my post."

Calvin engaged her request and was surprised with the strong, firm grip she had met him with. He walked briskly to the student foyer, he heard footsteps behind him.

"Can I make a request before class gets started?" Charlie had caught up with him and was now at his side. Not waiting on Calvin to reply, she continued, "I want to sit next to my girlfriend in your class. She's a hardhead but if I'm next to her, I can keep her in line."

"We'll talk about it next period. You need to get ready to go to your first class."

"Charlie!" Calvin heard Mrs. Clayborne interrupting them.

"Mrs. Clayborne, let me have a sip of what's in your cup?" Charlie reached for the coffee cup.

Calvin could smell the vodka and the Kaluha. The alcohol was rather strong and he knew that's the real reason Charlie wanted a sip from her cup. He shook his head at Mrs. Clayborne's boldness to drink in the presence of the students.

"No!" Mrs. Clayborne replied sharply. Charlie breathed in deeply and opened her mouth as if she could get a taste of the vapors from the drink, "you *cannot* have a sip of my coffee! And *no* you *cannot* sit next to your girlfriend in my third period class! You *know* you are *not* supposed to be on this side of the hall before the first bell rings in the morning. I tell ya', you better be glad I left my discipline referrals in my classroom or I'd send you to deal with Ms. Carter."

Charlie rolled her eyes. She put the earplugs back into her ears and walked off. Calvin faced Bonnie and smiled. He noticed that she started to look like the Easter Bunny with her bright blue eye shadow and rosy pink blush that seemed to age her by a couple of years. "That's how you get rid of those brats." Bonnie took a sip of her drink and rolled her eyes as well. "I wish that chick woulda had the gall to put her hands on me. I'd have her tail on the streets so fast. I can't stand those butch chicks who want to be more like men than the boys in my class. It's students like that that work my nerves."

Calvin watched as Bonnie moved like a decelerating train that barely made it to the next stop as she made her way to the other end of the student foyer by the gymnasium. He could picture the drama that she and Charlie were sure to have in her third period class and wondered if he would be able to hear her next door like she did the time before. Before he could ponder that thought anymore, the first bell rung and the students were allowed into the hallways to begin their first day of school.

The Rice Residence
8:45 AM

Maria made sure her husband was long gone, before she placed her call.

"This is Bilal speaking," her lover picked up the phone on the first ring. A smile appeared on her face she replayed images of the two of them doing some unholy things in the bedroom she shared with her husband.

"Good morning," Maria purred into the phone seductively. She adjusted herself on the love seat as she looked down at her plush lavender robe that felt as soft as cotton against her bare skin. She reached for a strand of her still drying hair, closed her eyes and twirled it like a shy sixteen-year-old speaking to her high school crush. "I was wondering if you could come by and see me."

"You know I can't do that, I've got some business to handle."

Disappointed, Maria smiled anyway as she thought about the moments she and Bilal shared before she met Calvin at the homeless shelter he was volunteering at when she first moved to Denver, Colorado. She was living at the center with an older man whom she convinced she would marry if he helped her come to America. That was a promise she broke the moment she saw Bilal walking down the street in his UPS uniform, sending her into a frenzy. Though she spoke English, Spanish and Portuguese fluently, sometimes, she'd play the role of not being able to speak English in order to manipulate people to get what she wanted. Recurring small talk after Bilal delivered supplies to the shelter, eventually led to a few dates and as she got to know the struggling college student, she hung with him pretty tight. The two used to be inseparable. As she got to know him, she found him to be smart, and witty.

It was Maria who'd convinced Bilal to apply for the personal banker job at Bank of America and to use the money from the job to finance his studies at the divinity school at Duke University. She wanted to make sure she kept tabs on her "investment."

"You mean you can't meet me somewhere and just hang out. Get a drink or something?"

"No, we can't, Maria," Bilal sounded agitated. "I like you as a person, but I respect the fact that you are married, so we can't do that anymore. Besides, I just came out of church, so I don't need to be thinking about that no way."

"Okay deacon," Maria tried to be coy on the phone, "I just wanted to give you an early Christmas present."

"You got me some money?" Bilal was laughing at his own joke. He knew the mere mention of cash would upset her. Maria knew he was pulling her string so she tried not to sound upset.

"I got a lotta money," Maria stretched out as she opened her robe. She noticed that she was wearing her wedding band and engagement ring and decided to take them off. Feeling the weight of her commitment decreasing, Maria felt open and free to continue in her adulterous flirtations, "do you have a lotta man?"

"See," Bilal was mad because Maria had turned the tables and started hitting on one of his sensitive spots. Bilal had the body that made women lust after him as if he were a shirtless model on the cover of a romance novel. "I know mine work, can't say the same for your husband." Maria conceded defeat on her man's ability to stay up as long as she wanted him to—and Bilal knew that because Maria had shared that tidbit of information with him. She often complained about her and Calvin's lack of lovemaking, their lack of time spent lovemaking, their lack of unity and togetherness. "When are you and Calvin coming to church with me?"

"As soon as I can keep him from kicking your butt—you know you can't take him on."

Bilal was so angry that he almost hung up the phone. Bilal could feel his throat tightening and suddenly struggled to breathe when he flashback to the night when Calvin started choking him after almost knocking his lights out after he'd spent the better part of the day on top of and inside of Maria. Bilal looked at the Bible that was on his desk as he was supposed to be searching for scriptures that went along with one of the Men's study classes that he was supposed to help moderate. "Why don't you come?"

"I want to really bad, but you just won't cooperate," she tried her best to sound seductive like Marylin Monroe.

"To church girl, I'm not talking about that." Too bad it didn't work. His flesh was beginning to fail him and the temptation to toss the Bible on the floor so he could stretch his legs and release himself to thoughts of Maria danced in his head. He turned his head to the left and looked at the cross and decided to fight the temptation. "Even if he don't want to come, you owe it to yourself and to the Lord to come to His house." Bilal smiled, glad that he was able to refocus the conversation away from sin.

"Boy please, you know you want me to hear you sing."

"I've given you plenty of private concerts already."

Maria was frustrated with Bilal, and sexually. "You know what I mean…well, why don't you sing me a Christmas carol?"

"Chestnuts roasting, on an open fire…" Bilal began to belt, reminding her of Otis from The Temptations.

"Oh Bilal, why don't you just come over for a few minutes? That's all I need is a few minutes."

"He's got lots of toys and goodies on his sleigh," Bilal continues to sing and laugh. "Naw, but for real. Surprise your husband. Do something exciting. It might be the last time you get to spend with him alone."

She knew he was telling the truth. Earlier this year, Calvin and Maria had talked about leaving for a getaway and spending Christmas and New Years in the Bahamas or Bermuda. They hadn't had a trip to themselves since their honeymoon three years ago.

"Aight, I'll get something together for him. I'm upset that I can't spend some time with you though," she sighed with a pout.

"Maria, you know the rules," Bilal reminded her, "When you married Calvin, you became taboo. Even if you were to divorce him, you and I could never be the same cause you married him in the first place."

Maria exhaled, "okay, I'll call you later on."

"Bye Maria."

Maria hung up the phone. She still couldn't figure out where or how she was going to get her sexual fix, but she knew that she needed to get it soon.

Chapter Thirteen

Monday, September 1, 2008
Lexington, NC (Riding on I-85 near the US 52 Exit)
4:45 PM

While D'Angelo was letting the woman of his dreams know that she was his "Lady," Calvin was contemplating how he was going to tell the woman sitting next to him the same thing. He and his wife had been having difficulties in their marriage off and on for the past two years and were just two steps away from a divorce. Calvin tried to reach out for her hand and was promptly dismissed. They stared at each other knowing the love that used to exist between them was starting to dwindle away. Calvin exhaled and reached for the radio and turned on the CD player. Toni Braxton started singing about how her man was "Trippin'" and Calvin was hoping that Maria got the message.

"How are we going to make this marriage work if you won't communicate with me?"

Maria started mumbling and complaining about her man in Portuguese in an attempt to get a negative rise out of him. She looked into Calvin's eyes and she couldn't believe that she had married or had kids with the murderer.

Calvin shook his head. He deeply inhaled the lavender scent from the air freshener that dangled from the rearview mirror. His eyes focused on traffic as he continued the drive to their counselor's office. Calvin initiated the marital counseling when he discovered that his wife had cheated on him with Bilal. When he walked in on their tryst, he had become heated—so heated that he had a flashback to the time in which he killed a man. He was twelve and living in Colorado at the time.

Calvin and his friends were being terrorized by a group of Crips. One of the terrorizers, Garfield, had killed his older sister, Carla, because she was dating a member of the Bloods gang. They were also jealous of the thriving candy business Calvin's friend, Martin ran. The money made selling sugar was enough for each member of the group of twelve to have pocket change. For months Garfield and his friends bullied and picked on Calvin and his friends. In the escalation of tension, Calvin stole a gun from one of the Bloods in the middle of an affray and challenged Garfield to a duel. Being fast with the fingers, Calvin shot off two bullets, killing Garfield before the boy could think to pull the trigger. Calvin had escaped prison because of the selflessness of Carlton. Carlton had taken the gun from Calvin after Garfield had dropped to the ground and shot at the dead body. When the police arrived at the scene, Carlton still had the gun in his hand and would later claim responsibility for the murder. Calvin had sworn that he'd never kill another person. Yet seeing another man on top of his woman that night, enjoying what should have been his and only his, almost caused him to renege on that promise. The only thing that kept him sane was the thought of Carlton getting out of jail soon. Calvin didn't want Carlton's prison sentence to be in vain by murdering again. Nothing would keep him from seeing his brother outside of prison walls, so he had kept his cool and let the adulterous deacon live.

Chapter Fourteen

Friday, August 29, 2008
Butler J. Parker High School – Mr. Rice's Class
8:45 AM

Calvin took a breather after having his first Individual Education Plan meeting for one of his learning disabled students. Usually, the Exceptional Children's Coordinator tried to hold off any IEP meetings, as they were called, until the end of the year but a parent could insist on having a meeting at any time. One had to be scheduled to accommodate a parent's request.

"Calvin! Hold up!"

Calvin was almost few feet for from his own classroom when he realized that Wes had addressed him in the hallway like a loud-ghetto dude from the projects. Usually it was he that chastised the students for not having enough manners and respect for the other students who were trying to learn.

Calvin smirked to himself at how hypocritical Wes was. It was days like this where Calvin hated coming to work because his planning period had been bombarded with nothing but meetings, meetings, meetings. He never understood why it seemed like he was the only academic teacher that the EC Coordinator could get in contact with to go to the meetings. Calvin was led to believe that every teacher was required to do one a semester so that the responsibility would be shared among all of the teachers. Truthfully, it seemed like the teachers who had first period planning and fourth period planning bore the brunt of that responsibility. Most parents seemed to schedule their meetings during those times.

Calvin finally addressed Wes, "man, you know we aren't in the streets." Calvin chastised Wes like Wes had done so many of the other students as they both entered his classroom.

"Man, please," Wes dismissed. Calvin smiled when he saw diamond pin under the cross of flap of Wes's dark gray Perry Ellis suite. Calvin had a matching one on in the same location of his sky-blue shirt.

"How are you going to tell the kids not to yell and run in the hallways when I'm sure everyone heard you shouting out my name as if we were at a rap concert?"

"Because I'm the assistant principal and these kids know I'm the boss, and I happen to be your boss."

"Yes Mr. Johnson, sir."

"Man look…" Wes pointed out some of students who were getting ready to enter Calvin's classroom to learn the day's lesson. Various students came in, engaged in their own conversations as they placed their bags on their seat and rushed to the flat screen Dell computer monitors to do their daily typing quiz that Calvin set up as a warm up and to help the students improve their typing skills. At nine o'clock in the morning, most of the students were starting their second class of the day with some going to lunch after their ninety minute session with Calvin was over. "I see that the students are on point. This is what makes my day right here."

Calvin nodded his head in this respect. In contrast, he saw two young ladies in the corner looking at a gossip website and talking about the latest scandal some rapper seemed to have found himself in. When one of the students caught his attention, Calvin quickly shook his head in disapproval, hoping not to have to write them up and send them out of the class for the day. School hadn't been in session for a whole day and the last thing he wanted to do was to send one of the students to detention before the week was out.

"The sooner you nip that in the bud, the better." Wes said, as he was about to leave. "I know you have talked to Sharice at least twice in my presence about her staying on task. Are you going to warn her about her behavior?"

Calvin looked at young girl whom he'd given a chance to— disappointed that she chose not to follow the directions that he'd written on the board that the other twenty seven students in his class seemed to follow. This had been Sharice's second time taking the Digital Communications class, having flunked last semester under Ms. Clayborne. Calvin didn't understand how a student who seemed like she had the potential to be valedictorian, obtained more discipline notices and trips to detention and in-school-suspensions than some of the more troublesome and violent students.

Calvin and Wes walked past a few students who rushed in the doors, trying not to be late before the nine o'clock bell rang out. He heard some comments mentioned about his meeting with him and subsequently with Miguel being moved to Friday evenings as opposed to Wednesdays.

"I thought we weren't going to start the action plan stuff until the middle of September." Calvin inquired about the sudden change in plans.

"It's nothing to worry about, bro. We decided to start earlier to give you more time to get acquainted with the program, especially since you are driving back and forth to A&T again this semester to finish the classes you need to complete the requirements for your teacher's license."

"Aight man, cool, let me get back to these students before they think they can get out of hand," Calvin re-entered the class leaving Wes to head back to his office. The bell rang and he noticed that Sharice was just putting a smart phone into her pocket. He noted that the gossip website was no longer on her computer monitor but the day's assignment being pulled up as he'd instructed her to do. Calvin shook his head—he knew he was going to have to deal with Sharice sooner or later but decided that he'd wait until the rest of the class got into their group assignments before he'd pull her aside to discuss her behavior.

Bilal's Bedroom
1:52 PM

Maria stared at her reflection in the mirror. The look of guilt crept upon her face when she saw Bilal's naked backside turn from his side to lying on his back and focused on the slight rising and falling of his chest as he lightly snored in his sleep. She was supposed to finish putting on a new coat of lipstick and inspecting her body to make sure that Bilal didn't leave any passion marks that would be a tale-tell sign of their affair. She took out a comb and quickly styled her long hair into a ponytail. As she stepped into her pants and high heels that she'd worn, the few extra inches gave her the height that would allow her to challenge Cheryl Swoopes or Lisa Leslie on the WNBA court.

Maria hated looking at her reflection. She could see an angel-like conscious stare back at her as if she were a character on a children's cartoon. She knew that she was risking everything to sleep with Bilal again. After calling his church to find out that he was free for the morning, she decided to call in sick to work and spend the morning frolicking with him. She'd made it to Bojangles to get his favorite Cajun biscuit breakfast with a bottle of orange juice. Then she surprised him as he was getting ready to walk out of the door and urged him to skip his morning jog and exercise routine at the fitness center and exercise her mind and body instead.

Just before she could turn away, another vision appeared before her—that of her deceased birth mother Rosa Vasquez-Boca. She hated the fact that as she was getting ready to bend down to pick up her blouse from the floor that she could see her mother staring back at her. Rosa cared more about being the mistress of the mayor of Goiânia, Brazil than being a mother to her and her younger sister, Avia. Their father, rather than live in the shame that his wife was continuing an affair with a prominent political figure and at the time, potential of president of Brazil, Michaelo Castanada Vasquez chose suicide before dishonor. The end result most likely ended with his soul burning in eternal damnation with the inability to ask for forgiveness for taking his own life. As much as Maria hated her mother, she hated even more admitting that she'd turn out to be just like her—except Maria never slept with a married man. *She* was, however, still married to Calvin and even though Bilal wasn't married, he was no more innocent because he knew that she *was* married.

Maria forcefully blew out her breath as she sought to escape the memories of her past that seemed to rush to the forefront of her mind. Her captor found only a few of the missing children, including Avia in the two days they had waited at the house. According to her captor, Avia was near death when she was found in the trunk of a beat up Cadillac.

The new captor would later move her to a house on the other end of Juarez—however, he would suffer the same fate as first one. Later, Maria and Avia were found with a few other children that were tied up in the closet and were taken to a nearby boarding home that was ran by the local Catholic church.

Maria decided that she wasn't going to take the chance of being captured and possibly worse again. She had already been raped—and if she could avoid that fate again, she'd be none the happier. Maria couldn't bring herself to trust the nuns, even though they appeared to be nice and the children of the home appeared to be well kept. So rather than live in a boarding house, she took a risk and with a young Avia in tow, decided to try their luck to get to America instead. Having a native Portuguese tongue had been a gateway to teaching herself Spanish which kept her from being a pawn by some pimp and her quick thinking allowed her to navigate the world of child prostitution. She used her body and its image to come up with money to buy bus rides, car hop and occasionally obtain temporary hiding places as she made her way back and forth from Juarez, Mexico to El Paso, Texas. It was in El Paso where she did the one thing she regretted to this day. After running into troubles with an underground drug lord whom had a fetish for young girls, she agreed to pawning of her ten year old sister's virginity. When the act was complete, the drug lord drove her ten miles south of Juarez to one of his houses where he made Maria and Avia perform unmentionable acts.

After their performance, the man refused to let them go, forcing Maria and Avia in bondage for six months. While based near Juarez, they were made to work farms and other menial child labor task that netted the drug lord extra money.

Maria's break came when a war broke out near their house and some of the men were shot dead as bullets hailed from inside and outside of her house. Maria had discovered a hidden shelter near the corner of the house where they were being held captive and instead of offering room for Avia to hide in as well, Maria chose to let Avia fend for herself. After a little more than a day, Maria could no longer tolerate the smell of death and climbed out of her shelter. She saw the bodies of some of her captures and quickly scanned the room to see if her sister was among the dead. When she didn't see Avia's body, she accepted one of two things—Avia either made it out alive and was either a slave or a servant to her new capture, or her sister had been murdered and had been given a burial of some sort. Deciding not to find out the answer, Maria continued her trek north until she was able to cross the Rio Grande river and stepped her foot back on Texas soil.

"What are you thinking about?" Bilal's voice interrupted her thoughts. As she turned around to face him, she noticed that he had the decency to conceal his nude body with the light brown sheets that couldn't stay on the bed while they were in the midst of their lust.

She hated when the thoughts of her mother and her sister seemed to overtake her mind. These thoughts seemed to come at the wrong-time-every-time she was getting ready leave Bilal's bed or rush Bilal out of her bed. Her conscious attacking her for past deeds and current ones was taking a toll on her body and her spirit. She looked down on his dresser and saw an open Bible verse and saw the scripture for Romans 13:13:

Let us walk honestly, as in the day; not in rioting and drunkenness, not in chambering and wantonness, not in strife and envying.

"How I can't wait to be your wife," she lied. The moment the words escaped her lips, she felt a sharp pang in her heart. She knew what she was doing was wrong and she didn't care. She thought it was funny that she was married to a man of faith and she was carrying on an affair with another man of faith and neither one of them could see that they were not equally yoked with her agnostic beliefs. The way she saw it, if God couldn't save her from prostitution and the harsh brutalities of forced child labor, then maybe He didn't exist.

"That would be nice," she felt Bilal's arms wrap around her waist. She looked in the mirror again and loved seeing his head rest against hers. She loved feeling of his body.

She rolled her eyes when he nuzzled on her neck.

"I'm on my way out," Maria turned cold. Even though she wouldn't have minded another game of "Twister" with him, she knew she would have to leave because it wouldn't be long before Calvin's last class ended and she wanted to be available in case he'd call.

"Oh—" Bilal sounded surprised. Maria looked in the mirror, saw the ghost of her mother standing next to her waving her finger in disapproval and Avia crying in the distance. She shook her head and her real mother and Avia disappeared. Maria watched in the mirror as Bilal walked into the bathroom in his master bedroom. On the left, next to the dresser, she found it odd that Bilal would hang a framed copy of his Bachelors of Science in Finance from North Carolina Central University and his Masters of Business Administration degree from the University of North Carolina-Greensboro hanging one on top of the other next to a framed picture of the Ten Commandments. Below, she saw the Apple computer and the Peachtree and Quicken software that she assumed he used to do work from home. She moved the mouse and was surprised that the computer wasn't password protected but when she saw the time on the clock, she knew that she needed to get out of the apartment.

Maria walked to the bathroom and stood at the doorway and adored his nakedness. A part of her wanted to strip her clothes off and join him but she knew she couldn't do that. Instead, she blew him a kiss and left his bedroom.

As she left Bilal's apartment which was on the corner of Second and Marshall in downtown Winston-Salem, she knew she only had about fifteen minutes to get from his spot to the house she shared with Calvin. Even though she didn't expect Calvin to come home for another hour or so, she also didn't want to be caught off guard on a rare day he was able to leave when the students left.

Friday, August 29, 2008

Miguel's Classroom
2:30 PM

The bell rang and Calvin was happy that the first week of school had gone without incident. Charlie proved to be the real comedienne in his second period class. Between her and Sharice's addiction to blogs and other gossip sites not pertaining to Digital Communications, he knew that his first class of the day would prove to be a challenge. He was happy that the students seemed to embrace using skeleton PowerPoint slides as a basis for notes that he had for different input and handheld devices. The essential questions Calvin created that outlined what the topic for the day's discussion appeared to be great lead-ins for his lectures that kept his students actively engaged.

A few times, Calvin had to encourage some of the students to speak up and to elaborate on the information that they learned and to avoid reading directly from the PowerPoint as they present the material. Dr. Hewett surprised Calvin by coming into the classroom during Calvin's third period and offered constructive criticism about classroom instruction and the way his lesson plans had been structured.

In the next few minutes, Calvin knew that he would have a meeting with Wes to discuss his progress as he worked on the action plan program. When he stepped in and took a seat, Calvin felt like he was stepping into a gripe session instead of receiving help and improvement tips.

He was surprised when he found out that Dr. Hewett was turning in an evaluation on his class performance so soon. It was the first week of school and students were getting used to being back in school and the teachers were still learning their students' strengths and weaknesses so they could set their strategies accordingly. It didn't seem fair to him that he was being evaluated when the students hadn't had a chance to mesh well with him or the curriculum.

The meeting with Miguel was less stressful. Calvin got a chance to relay some of the concerns that Wes seemed to have all of a sudden. Miguel would respond with ideas and demonstrate a few teaching techniques that he thought could work with Calvin's class. Then at the end of their meeting, Calvin and Miguel signed a couple of documents proving that they did meet at their appointed time so that Calvin could keep a copy in the mentor folder he was expected to keep during his first three years as a teacher.

Miguel encouraged Calvin to enjoy the weekend and to leave Butler J. Parker stress in Concord and for him to enjoy the weekend with his wife. Calvin was a few steps ahead of him as he was looking forward to getting some take out from Q'Doba, the Mexican grill takeout restaurant on Hanes Mall Boulevard. He also wanted to escape from their house to a master suite in the Holiday Inn on Stratford Road near the I-40 exit. Calvin wanted Maria to be locked in and pampered to for the weekend without having to leave town. On this mini-honeymoon, he'd hoped he'd be able to rekindle some spontaneous romance that seemed to be lacking in their love life and just spend the weekend with his wife uninterrupted.

Chapter Fifteen

Wednesday, September 3, 2008
Charlotte Douglass International Airport
11:00 AM

"Man, where you at?" Wes turned around to see Shelby, his favorite white boy, trailing behind him and acting hood. Calvin noticed the surprised looks on some of the patron's faces as they walked through the airport.

Calvin agreed to tag along with Wes as an opportunity to hang out with him outside of work. Ever since Wes became Calvin's boss, they've rarely hung out outside of work. Calvin remembered meeting Shelby at the CIAA in tournament in Winston-Salem. He had pledged the same fraternity at Norfolk State University.

Shelby had shared with him that his grandfather was black and that it was his grandfather's sister raised him and his older brother in a rundown house in Hampton, Virginia. And despite the fact he looked like his European ancestors, Shelby identified as black. That Sunday, after they'd gone to church together, Calvin got to know Shelby. He found out that his aunt fed him chitterlings, greens, cornbread and other traditional staples found in a lower class black family home. Shelby also knew what it was like to fight cockroaches for his cereal and rats for a cube of cheese.

After graduation, Shelby had gotten a job at BB&T's IT department and Calvin started out as a financial services officer.

Shortly after BB&T bought a bank in Virginia, Shelby had to go back to his stomping grounds, but that didn't stop him from visiting Calvin often.

Calvin reached back and gave Shelby a one arm hug, "I can't believe you are acting a fool with Wes."

"You should be worried about how I'm gonna act a fool." Shelby boasted and Calvin couldn't help but laugh. Shelby may have grown up in the hood, but he still sounded like Garth Brooks. But don't get it twisted, Calvin was the only one that could laugh at the twang in his voice. Anyone else would find that they'd have four lips instead of two if so much as a grin crept on their face. "I see you let this dude con you into teaching these kids."

"Someone's gotta do it," Calvin conceded.

"There's nothing wrong with being a teacher." Wes defended. "We just need a break every now and then."

"You wouldn't know unless you stepped back in the classroom," Calvin almost regretted saying.

Shelby was far from ugly. He resembled Van Diesel with his sandy, spiked low cut hair, toned shoulders, naturally bronzed skin and light brown eyes. Calvin saw firsthand how plenty of women flocked to him and mistake him for a light-skinned black dude. As they walked through the terminal, Calvin noticed how the women kept their eyes peeled on the three of them.

"I respect the two of y'all for stepping in the classroom. I couldn't do it. If one those kids got in my face, I'd lay'em flat," Shelby stopped for a second to entertain one of the ladies who'd approached him. Shelby pulled out his phone, took her number and gave her a kiss on the cheek.

Calvin shook his head as Shelby and Wes continued their vulgar and crude tirade on the way to baggage claim. Once Shelby got his belongings, they walked to the drop off section where Wes paid a pretty penny to keep have a black stretch

Escalade limo waiting on them. The three of them stepped in and rode in silence as they made their trip to Dave and Buster's.

"You know what I want to do," Shelby interrupted the quietness that had overtaken the ride home. "I want to go to a Bible study. I haven't been to church or had a prayer in a long time."

Wes looked at Shelby like he was crazy. "Are you sure? You just got to North Carolina and the first thing you want to do is go to a church."

"Yeah man—let's face it. God could come back tomorrow and I had too much fun on that plane that I need to repent for and get right. You never know when your time to go is going to be and you want to make that investment now before you miss out on a great opportunity."

Calvin shook his head as he could imagine what kind of fun Shelby and one of the stewardess had no business having as part of the mile-high club.

"Man—I was hoping to take you to Crave and get a hookah."

Calvin's face twisted up, "since when do you smoke hookahs?"

"Last year, I discovered them on my trip to India."

In the back of his mind, Miguel's warning came to mind.

Friday, September 12, 2008
Miguel's Classroom
11:00 AM

Calvin sat in on an observation of Reverend Conseco's class. She was a Bible Studies teacher who shared a room with Miguel. Calvin found her to be a motivator as they shifted through the Word and he confided in her about his spiritual journey. He'd taken notes to go along with an assignment he had at A&T needed to have completed.

"Mr. Rice," Calvin turned his head when he saw one of his second period students, Austin Texas, calling his name. Calvin noticed the flaco-framed young man whose wire-rimmed glasses matched his physique.

"Austin, what's going on?" He asked as the young man whom had caught up with him. Calvin and Austin would have to walk to the other end of the hallway to get to his class.

"I'm hanging in there—that and trying to stay away from Charlie."

As the boy spoke the devil's name, Calvin saw her with her pants hanging off of her behind. She exposed her Carolina blue boxers with the school's logo spread throughout the clothing.

"What's Charlie doing to you?" Calvin ignored the sight and focused on Austin.

"Blackmail."

Calvin looked at him. He wanted to say something else but instead he asked, "what would she have to blackmail you on?"

"If I told you—you wouldn't believe it. But she got proof and that's why she's running this school."

Hmm, Calvin thought, trying to see where this information was going to be useful to him later on. He'd met Austin's mother and father during orientation and they reminded him that if he was ever in trouble that he was more than welcomed to call them at home or at work anytime. The thought crossed his mind to test that theory but he decided that he'd wait until he knew what the piece of information was.

"Austin, let me talk to you for a minute…" Charlie called out to him. She looked at Calvin and then looked at Austin. Austin dropped his head down as if he were guilty of something. "Come on, I don't bite," Charlie continued as she opened her mouth and chomped down on air. Austin followed her direction and Calvin went inside the classroom and grabbed the box of headphones with the microphone attached to them. As the students' trickled into the classroom, he made sure that each student would have one.

"Hello *Mr. Rice*," Chante waddled into the classroom. The smart and attractive junior was seven months pregnant with her third baby and she loved to flirt with Calvin every chance she got. He typically ignored her advances because he had no intentions of being baby father number four. It was rumored that the baby she was carrying belonged to one of the football coaches at the school.

"Good morning Chante. Go ahead and set the computer up and then have a seat at your desk so that you may hear the instructions."

Chante pouted, "I was hoping we'd talk about the re-run of *College Hill* or the new Nikki Turner book I'm reading."

Calvin watched as she placed her bags down and then with some assistance from Charlie, waddled to her computer.

"Mr. Rice," Otey Ramiz, his freshman class clown and unofficial microphone shouted as he walked into the door, "are we going to get on the internet today?"

"Maybe, if you can do it with your speech recognition system that we will be working with today."

"Dah—I mean bummer," Otey said as he snatch the headphones from him. "I wanted to listen to that new Lil' Wayne."

"You can't get 'a mili' if you don't do your work. I'm sure Lil' Wayne knows how to operate a speech recognition device."

Otey rolled his eyes and took his seat. Calvin shook his head. Calvin looked at the clock and was surprised that Emily Hunt, Omarion Johnson, Shad Moses and Kobe Carter sprinting to his room as if it were in the last stretch marathon.

"Walk, don't run," Calvin warned, "or I'll send all of you back to the end of the hallway and make you walk again."

"Oh God!" Emily huffed as she came to a complete stop. She moved the hair from her face.

"And don't use my Lord and Savior's name in vain."

"But Rice, why can't we just get along? Anyway," she replied in the same manner that her best friend, Chante would. "Come on Omarion, let's hurry up so we can get our seats next to Chante. We'll read *Lil' Red Riding Hood* to you once we finish these assignments."

Omarion licked his lips and slowed down so he could watch Emily walk away. Every time Calvin saw him, Omarion had his arms around some white girl. Being the star football player, he had as many girls and some grown women that he could handle. But Emily wouldn't give him the time of day. One thing he'd always respect about Emily was that she'd stand up to anyone, even to Charlie. Charlie could beat the breaks off of Emily over and over again and Emily would still stand her ground.

"We'll get in some of the reading assignments too," Calvin told Omarion. For one of his graduate classes, he made a commitment for helping his Omarion learn to read. It was a shame he was supposed to graduate this year and Omarion could barely spell his name.

"I just wanna rap, I just wanna sing. I wish Calvin would stop trippin' let me do my own thing," Shad spit bars like he was at a rap concert.

"Excuse me," Calvin stopped him by putting his hand on his shoulder.

"See, this is what I'm talking about." Shad shoved Calvin's hand off of him.

"It's Mr. Rice, Shad," Calvin reminded him for the umpteenth time.

"I know what your name is."

"And I know you can't rap like Bow Wow, so you might as well quit while you're ahead." Calvin put the headphones in his hand.

"Man, you get on my nerves. Bow Wow and I got the same name, and I'm going to be a bigger star than he is one day too."

"No, your name is *close* to his, but you don't have the skills he got. Maybe if you practice a lil' more after school, *after* you do your homework, you can get on his level. Besides, his mama stayed on him about his school work and he made good grades to stay in the industry, maybe you should try that."

Shad pretended like he didn't hear him and took his seat next to Charlie.

"Mr. Rice, let me go to the bathroom real quick." Kobe said as he took the headphones from Calvin's hand and rushed to put his backpack at his seat.

"Boy, you just had five minutes to do what you need to do."

"Come on Mr. Rice, five minutes is not enough time for me to take a leak and then get pretty enough to keep my swag on for the ladies."

"Maybe you need to learn to improve your game."

"I'm always improving."

The bell rang and just as Calvin was getting ready to close the door, Evelyn Carter walked in with a clipboard in hand and quickly took a seat near the back of the room. Her face was stoic and a noticeable change in Kobe's attitude was apparent. Calvin thought it was funny how Kobe would act one way when his mother was in the classroom and another when she was nowhere around.

Ten minutes after class had begun and the students had just finished their warm up typing lesson on the computer. Calvin hadn't expected his second evaluation to take place so soon, but nevertheless he was prepared. He watched as a few students walked up to her and hug her as if they were hugging their own grandmother before warning them that they still had a lecture and an assessment to get through.

As some of the students work through the program, Calvin pointed out how the programs fail to recognize some people's voices if they spoke too fast or if their voice was really raspy. He looked at Evelyn and noticed that her nose was into the pad and whatever it was she was writing about him. Calvin made sure to reference the bulletin board that he turned into a "word wall" to go over key vocabulary words that the students needed to know for his class.

Looking at the clock, he noticed that the students were on task and maneuvering their way through the program on their own with little need of assistance. Omarion took his place at the desk and Calvin met him at the center of the class room. Omarion took out the flashcards he was working on that had a mixture of words from his English class and the words from the word wall. Calvin helped Omarion build sentences using all of the words. That's when he saw her looking at him with a confused look.

Calvin continued working with Omarion until five minutes before class was to end. He called everyone to their seats and then he reviewed the word wall and the concepts of the speech recognition program with everyone. Satisfied that the students were able to answer the questions without assistance, he let them work independently on their long term class project.

"I see you are using the word wall," Evelyn pointed out as the class was being dismissed by the bell.

"I try to use every tool available to make sure that the students grasp keywords and can master the concepts so they can be successful on the assessments."

Calvin handed her a copy of his lesson plans and Evelyn shook her head as she left the classroom.

The Rice Residence
3:00 PM

Maria weighed her options and decided that it was best for her to get out of the marriage. She hadn't loved Calvin for some time and she knew that she would not be happy if she continued to live with him. She wanted a divorce and she was willing to do it at any cost.

She also didn't want to risk Calvin getting angry enough to kill Bilal, so she decided that she would surprise him. She had a nice veggie lasagna meal prepare for Calvin—one of his favorites—complete with a strawberry and spinach balsamic salad and red wine. Maria made arrangements with a drug dealer friend of hers to get one of the popular "date rape" drugs, and she meticulously followed the written instructions that was provided as she blended it in to his drink.

Upon Calvin's arriving home, she made sure she was spontaneous and gave him something he could feel while Aretha was singing one of her most famous tunes in the background. When they were done with their grownup games, she decided it was best if she listened to Beyonce, Kelly, and Michelle's advice and catered to her man by feeding him on the couch as she sat in his lap. She continued her role as the innocent housewife as she waited for the drug to take effect. Once Calvin was out cold, she called Bilal.

"It's done."

"Really? You told him you want a divorce?" Bilal got excited. "You told him you wanted to be with me?"

"I didn't have to say that but he got the message. Can you pick me up as soon as possible?"

"I'll be there in ten minutes," Bilal replied and hung up the phone.

Maria went to the desk and she quickly composed her Dear John Letter informing Calvin of the reasons why she wanted a divorce. Then she rushed upstairs and threw all the clothes that she thought would fit in a bag and she grabbed her credit cards and some cash. She also made a mental note to search for a pawn shop so she could get cash for her engagement ring and wedding band.

As soon as the doorbell rang, Maria opened the door and Bilal immediately made himself useful by helping Maria carry Calvin and put him in bed. Maria placed her letter on the pillow feeling a slight tinge of guilt as she thought about the fact that Calvin's brother was getting out of jail soon.

She knew Calvin was especially excited because Carlton expressed interest in joining the Street Disciples Ministry and passing out copies of *The Upper Room* to sinners and saints on Dr. Martin Luther King Boulevard. Maria loved watching the men dressed in street clothes as they talked about the Lord. She was particularly fond of Donte Speaks, who in his past life was a successful adult video star. She thought of the five foot ten sexy young thang and all of the videos she wished she had made with him before he retired.

"We need to go," Bilal was firm in his command as he gently grabbed her hand and led her out of the room she shared with her husband. When she looked at Bilal and thought of the money and the great sex she had with him, she felt confident that her decision to leave him was the right one.

Chapter Sixteen

Saturday, September 13, 2008
Rice Residence
12:00 PM

"Say it again," Faith was singing an old Aretha Franklin tune. Sort of sounds like her, in a way. Calvin couldn't believe that Rahliem had brought her along to help him find Maria. It had been some time since he seen her outside of service. Calvin had been so caught up in what was going on with his schooling and his teaching and his wife—he'd forgotten that Rahliem was engaged.

And just like the typical church lady, she was dressed to impress. She was wearing a red business suit and skirt, with a yellow band around the waist, with the hat to match. The hat was an impressive design within itself, with a yellow flower sticking out of it with red speckles.

"I can't believe she left me this letter—I deserve better than that," Calvin vented as he read the letter over again. Rahliem took the letter from him, folded it and put it in his pocket.

"What you do that for?"

"Because I want you to discover whether finding your wife and reconciling is in God's will." Rahliem said has he took out his pocket Bible and handed it to Calvin. "I want you to read Proverbs 5:1-23."

Calvin took the book from him then scrunched his lips. "That's the whole chapter."

"You say that as if I asked you to read the whole Bible," Rahliem replied.

Calvin read the chapter aloud. "This must be your way of telling me to stop looking for her."

"No—actually, that was the instruction God just placed on my heart to give to you. I'm glad you listened."

Calvin was happy to see that Rahliem hadn't changed a bit. Despite being a leader of a church group, Rahliem still had a comedic side to him.

"It's not that easy."

"I never said it was going to be."

Rahliem turned the radio from the smooth R&B and classic soul FM station to WAAA AM, which was the locally-owned classic soul, blues and gospel station. Yolanda Adams was singing about the battle being the Lord's. Calvin wasn't always used to that. He was always used to being able to facing his problems head on and finding solutions. Even after he got saved—he figured that if he handled some of his other problems, he wouldn't stress the Lord out on some of his small issues.

Saturday, September 13, 2008
Rice Residence
11:57 PM

Calvin had a dream.

Maria was sleeping in the bed next to him just like a little baby. He sat up in the bed and stared at her—praising God for blessing him with a woman that was just for him. Maria was just as beautiful as the day they eloped three years ago; she's just as beautiful as the day he met her when he was sixteen.

Calvin had met Maria almost ten years ago when she was staying at a homeless shelter with his cousin, Juan. Calvin saw

Maria as she was washing clothes and he knew that his life was going to change forever.

As he continued to admire the woman that was his rib, he silently confessed to God that he had given up a lot to be with her. His parents were upset that he'd chosen a Latina to marry. His younger brother had admitted to lusting after her, which had been a thorn in their relationship. But Maria, along with the help of his youth psychiatrist, was able to help free him from the nightmares he had of being chased by Garfield's living relatives.

Calvin had to admit that Maria also had given him more chances than he probably deserved as well. Once he'd given his virginity to her after six months of dating, he regretted that he lied about being eighteen. His being a few weeks shy of his sixteenth birthday put the young illegal immigrant at risk for being jailed for inappropriate sexual acts with a minor.

When they broke up the first time, he wished that he'd held out instead of enjoying his sexual freedom that came with being a freshman in college.

Maria should have been number one in everything in his life —except after God. When he was offered an academic scholarship from Winston-Salem State University, he jumped at the opportunity to go across the country. Calvin joined his best friend, Martin at the same school. He left Maria in Denver to fend for herself. He couldn't afford to bring her with him at the time.

Once he did—there were the miscarriages and the frustration they caused. Calvin couldn't wait until they had children together, but every time they tried—they failed. Calvin and Maria talked about adopting but his urge to have *his own* flesh and blood often put pressure on their relationship. Maria accused Calvin for wanting his own children for bragging rights and for carrying *his* genes.

Then there were the trips to the infertility clinic that couldn't deem him infertile, but suggested his low sperm count was a contributing factor to their low success rate. With the miscarriages —Calvin figured his count couldn't be *that* low. Ironically after each miscarriage it just made Calvin that determined to want children more.

Calvin awaken, wishing that Maria was on her side of the bed but found it empty. Maria was gone and Bilal had taken him from her. He couldn't find them and that wrecked his whole world— turning him into the man he didn't want him to be again.

Calvin picked up his Bible and read Psalm 23 and 24 and found himself drifting into sleep again—dreaming about Maria, again.

Chapter Seventeen

Friday, September 12, 2008
Cafeteria – Butler J. Parker High
11:57 AM

The jerk chicken looked appetizing as it sat next to the ackee and salt fish, fried plantains, fried dumplings, rice and peas, gizzada and potato pudding. Calvin had grabbed a can of Irish Moss that was next to hot chocolate and limeade drinks. The cafeteria workers set out the Jamaican food for the staff day luncheon, which left one of the workers crying in tears off to the side as she was being honored with foods from her home land. The last time Calvin remembered having a table full of Jamaican food had be the year he we won the election to be Mr. Ram at WSSU.

Calvin and all of the other teachers were stuck in another workshop as the students were enjoying another day off. Having great food from an island many dreamed about visiting made the work day worth it.

"I wish I could take this food home," Calvin murmured. There weren't any known Jamaican restaurants in Winston-Salem and he didn't want to travel to the ones in Charlotte and then head back north. He tried that one time and the food got cold and didn't taste as good.

"I swear the students get more days off than I get, and I have enough vacation time to retire a full year early." Mrs. Clayborne complained as she put a heaping spoonful of the rice and peas on her plate.

Mrs. Clayborne reeked of strong Bourbon and whiskey. A trace of marijuana escaped her breath as she turned to face Calvin. The Jamaican food that had him at a state of ecstasy had to take a back seat as he was forced to deal with the reality. No more "getting her groove back" dreams of him being Winston and Maria being Stella.

I can't believe she's so high, Calvin noted to himself as he continued down the line to get more food on his plate. "I was thinking the same thing," Calvin commented to keep the conversation going. He knew that Mrs. Clayborne really needed someone to talk to and talking couldn't get him in trouble, he thought.

"When I first started teaching, we didn't get all of these teacher workdays during the year or workshops. Now it seems like we are learning new teaching strategies every week."

"Awe cheer up," Miguel brought his plate and followed them in line. Calvin looked at his plate and noticed that it was equally appetizing as his. "We need time to be around grown folks for a change—let the kids stay home."

Once Calvin, Miguel and Mrs. Clayborne worked through the line, they noticed that different teachers were sitting together with their departments. The CTE department had the far table in the corner away from the food. Calvin and the gang joined them.

They sat down and Calvin said a blessing over the food. When he looked up, he noticed Mrs. Clayborne staring off into space and that Miguel was still in prayer. Reverend Conseco smiled, "thank you for blessing the food," she said.

"You're welcome."

Calvin dug into the jerk chicken and just as he suspected, the food was delicious—not to spicy and grilled just right.

"Man this food is banging," Wes hopped into the empty seat next to Calvin. "So how are you enjoying the workshop so far?"

"It's okay." Calvin responded, not trying to stay on the subject too long.

"I think that it's a waste of time," Mrs. Clayborne said. "Just like praying before you eat."

"Awe come on," Miguel was irritated.

"No, let's hear her out," Wes encourage, "why do you think prayer before eating is a waste of time?"

"Because, God isn't real." Mrs. Clayborne started. "if God was real, we wouldn't have the problems in the schools do now."

That was it, Calvin said to himself. *That was the reason why she didn't believe that any of the students had any hope or the ability to get better. That's why she didn't care.*

Calvin never saw it that way before. Of course, he knew there were people who weren't saved. People who couldn't wrap their mind that Jesus Christ gave his life on the cross so that they wouldn't have to atone for their sins. That Jesus forgave them. But at times, Calvin feigned naiveté and wanted to believe that everyone and their mama was saved. Believe that more souls just needed to return to Christ after they lost their way.

Never had he had a close encounter with an atheist before.

"I believe the reason why we are having so much problems and chaos is because we have removed prayer from schools," Miguel countered, bringing Calvin's mind back to focus. "When we lost the battle to keep prayer in schools and to a point, Jesus in the forefront—it was like we told our Lord and Savior to get the hell out of here. And unfortunately for us, He left rather quickly."

"Oh my gosh, you are a nut-job," Mrs. Clayborne mumbled.

"I beg to differ." Reverend Conseco interjected it. "I feel that we didn't have an increase of student violence, school bombings and shoots and the like until prayer no longer became mandatory in schools."

"I don't let no one stop me from praying." Wes said.

Yes, Calvin cheered. *Miguel will finally see that Wes is a Christian.*

"I don't either," Calvin stated. "I read verses from the Bible before I start some of my classes—especially second period."

Small chuckles and laughter to could be heard at the table. "And when I get the chance, I drop in on Reverend Conseco's classes just so I can hear the Word."

"But God is not mutually exclusive to the Bible," Wes pointed out.

Err—where did this come from, Calvin was confused. The Wes he went to college with would've never made a statement like that.

"What do you mean?" Miguel egged him on as if he were instigating a snap battle.

"I mean that I chant and I hymn. I get into my daily affirmations and my favorite quotes and sayings. And I read the Bible too—sometimes," Wes confirmed.

"But the Bible says that Jesus is the way, the truth and the light," Calvin spoke up.

"The Bible was written by man and I wish we would just finally admit that, for once." Mrs. Clayborne was getting increasingly frustrated.

Calvin could understand why. He, Miguel and Reverend Conseco all agreed that Jesus Christ came so that mankind could be saved. That's why he got on the cross—suffered, bled and died for. That's what he gave his life for.

"The Bible was written by man, but inspired by God," Miguel corrected.

"Yeah, after a few drinks and a hitting up the bong a few times—the Bible is the best fiction novel ever." Mrs. Clayborne spoke ignorantly. "I'll have to keep that in mind the next time I get into one of the gospels." Mrs. Clayborne stood up and grabbed her tray. "It's almost time for the next session to begin.

I'm going to have to eat my lunch elsewhere, so that I may have some time with myself."

"I gotta go too," Wes offered as he got up. "I need to interact with the other teachers but this was a good discussion on God and we need to have them more often. Maybe next time, I can show you some material I found Calvin."

Calvin didn't know what to say so he said nothing but shake his head. He watched as Wes walked away and he couldn't believe that Wes could believe that there was more than one path to God. The Bible clearly stated otherwise.

"And see," Reverend Conseco brought the conversation back to their table. "This is why we need to bring prayer back to school. Christianity is under attack and if we are not careful, we will lose this generation before us to free-minded thinking like this."

"I agree," Calvin said as he took a bit of his jerk chicken. Fortunately, the food was still warm, but his spirit became more concerned about Wes as the seconds went on. Calvin decided to let Wes know that the invitation to attend his church still stood. Calvin was determined to use that time to find out what this chanting was about and whom Wes was chanting to.

Chapter Eighteen

Tuesday, September 16, 2008
Mr. Rice's Classroom – Butler J. Parker High
2:45 PM

Second block ran much smoothly than it had in the first two weeks. The power struggle seemed to have minimized a little bit. Calvin took steps to rearrange the seating chart and call on students to participate in class more. Calvin called the students randomly to answer questions and incorporated some of the music they liked to listen to as well as infusing cultural diversity with the music selection.

Calvin chose introduction videos that were somewhat entertaining, but allowed him to get a social conscious message across about how business was conducted and how their behaviors either further their aims or hurt them. One of the Exceptional Children's teachers started to make more visits in this class to check on him and the students. They are a welcome guest as having been a community support specialist—Calvin had worked as a teacher's aide and a direct care worker so he knew what it is like having to work with the students in a class setting. Calvin had excelled in working with students one on one and can curb individual behaviors and that was one of his motivators for becoming a teacher. Dealing with as many as five students who have various treatment plans and in a wide range of ages and maturity present a different challenge, but one he was willing to face head on.

Calvin gave a quiz on the parts of the computer and the viruses and identifying the labels and alternative input devices. He ended up failing eight of the students because they talked throughout the whole test. In several of the modifications that the students had in their education plans, he was required to give the students the whole class period to do a test or a quiz and he asked for the students to be quiet and not get on games or videos.

Calvin figured the students decided that they were going to test him. When he returned their grades back with zeros, some of the students were upset and threatened to get him fired. Some students got the hint that he was serious and that they were not going to be able to run over him like they had some of their other teachers.

That was the story all last week too—the students wanted to type and play video games. Calvin laid out the ground rules on the first day of the semester, handed out copies of the classroom expectations and the rules for computer use. The students complained about having their parents sign and return the forms.

The key to keeping the students in check would depend on Calvin enforcing the classroom policies early on so that other students would know that his was not a class where they can dome in a do what they want to do.

Surprisingly, third block faired much better with only two students receiving zeros for talking during the test. The grades in this class were also higher as they worked to try to be more interactive in class and asked more questions when they don't understand something.

Calvin had no problems in fourth block during the quiz. Almost all the students passed with a D or better. The students were interested in moving beyond computer parts and devices and had even found ways that the devices were used to produce and transmit data they needed in their personal lives. With Calvin's fourth block, he had learned that some of the students were on various medications or receiving Exceptional Children's services. This class was milder compared to the first two, but they are also ready to go home and are counting the clock.

At the end of class, Calvin was getting his notes together for the second part of the Thinking Maps workshop he had to attend. When he looked up, he saw Miguel at the door.

"You ready?"

"As ready as I'm going to be."

"Yeah," Miguel stalled has he came in to take a seat. "But you get them out of the way now, you don't have to deal with them throughout the week."

Calvin shook his head.

"Is dealing with your students getting any better?"

"Yeah and no—I think all those zeros let them know I mean business."

"Good, never let your guard down."

"I know. I see that now more than ever."

"So what do you think about the Thinking Maps workshop? How do you see using the maps to connect the main idea to the sub ideas that you are talking about being useful in your class?"

"For me, it's similar to the program Winston-Salem/Forsyth County Schools uses called Balanced Literacy for their middle schools. They start the class with an Essential Question which is what they hope the students learn at the end of the day. Then the teachers navigate the students through a guided practice and lead them to their independent student activities. The Thinking Maps program uses some of the same techniques as Balanced Literacy but their focus is on using maps to connect ideas and concepts in the subjects."

"That's nice—I'm glad you go the concept. Don't forget, your Smart Board training is tomorrow."

"I need that. I need to learn how to cut and paste and how to write on the board and convert my writings into text. And I still need to play with the technology a little bit so I can get better aquatinted with it and so I can come up with more ideas on how to talk about the Smart Board as being input device."

"You didn't use the Smart Board last year?"

"No. The school I was at last year didn't have it and when I came to Butler last semester, there was no time to teach me how to use the device."

"That was bad follow up on my part. But I tell you what, when you come to my class on Friday, I'll make sure I point out what I'm doing so that you can use the tools in future classes. That way, by the time you have the interest meeting for FBLA, you'll be on point with it."

Calvin had almost forgotten about FBLA—Future Business Leaders of America. When Butler J. Parker opened seven years ago, they had a chapter but after a couple of years, the organization had fallen to the wayside. Calvin's goal was to reactivate the chapter and to at least participate in some competitions and other business events in the Concord and Charlotte areas.

"That sounds like a plan," Calvin looked at the time on the computer. He and Miguel had five minutes to get to the cafeteria where the workshop was going to be held. "We need to get going."

Calvin secured the computer and made sure all twenty-four monitors were off. Satisfied, he followed Miguel out of the room and headed to another long, three hour after school workshop.

Chapter Nineteen

Friday, September 19, 2008
Mr. Rice's Classroom – Butler J. Parker High
12:00 PM

Calvin decided that this day, he'd let the students get what a hands on experience with the devices before the test on Monday.

For the last three weeks, he'd been handling new school business and helping the students learn more about the devices and now was the time to get out of this short unit and pull it together. A couple of the students had brought their ten dollar fees the school system charged for the personal headsets that would be used in the speech recognition unit that Calvin would be teaching toward the end of the semester.

"Mr. Rice," one of the students called him. Calvin noticed that when Austin called his name, he had tears in his eyes. He hadn't even noticed that the young man had been crying and he felt some kind of way about that. Calvin silently motioned the young man to the front. "My mother died last night."

Calvin could see the tear drop as it slowly rolled from Austin's face to Calvin's desk.

"He's telling the truth." Emily vouched. "I told him to stay home today but he said he can't deal with his father."

"Yeah, Mrs. Texas was a good woman." Charlie said.

Calvin found himself altering the lesson to help Austin and the rest of the class deal with his mother's death. He didn't know that many of the students in his class knew Austin's mother.

Calvin wasn't insensitive—and even though he still had both of his parent's, he wanted to show some compassion. He was glad that the two objectives he planned to work on this day were light because he would need to give his students time to adjust and support their friend.

As Austin took time to grieve, he still tried to follow the lesson, taking advantage of the opportunity to gain "hands on" experience with various handheld devices such as PDA's, digital and video cameras and interactive white boards. The presentations they did yesterday went really well and he was looking forward finish grading their tests.

One of the tests had been completed and Calvin still had two more classes to grade. Calvin decided that he would have to make a few modifications to the teaching schedule due to changes on when progress reports go out. As a result, one of the quizzes the students were supposed to take next week, they did not get a chance to work on, so they would have to push the material up.

He'd hoped the class would take the time to discover all that the devices could do on their own without constant monitoring and intervention. His second period had done a wonderful job with that with no redirection whatsoever.

"Otey and Omarion, do not throw the PDA's please."

Calvin should have taken the device and wrote both of them up, but he wasn't in the mood to deal with any drama.

"Why shouldn't I throw the PDA?" Otey challenged him.

His defiance was changing the mood of the class and the last thing Calvin wanted was to be bothered with a disobedient student. But what was he to do.

"I should throw the device at you and see if I can knock your head off with it."

"Come again," Calvin almost forgot that he wasn't on the streets—wasn't that twelve year old boy who'd answer a challenge and not hesitate to throw two dukes up at a moment's notice.

"I said I should knock your head off with the thing."

"Why don't you go to detention?" Calvin suggested, filling out the form with anticipation of getting the student out of class and preventing any other disruption.

Otey got up and walked to the other side of the desk, "you know if I come up to that desk, it's gonna be me and you son, me and you."

"Ooh, we get to see a fight." Chante got excited.

"No, it's not going to be me and you—you are getting ready to leave—"

"I'm not getting ready to go nowhere," Otey declared and proceeded to called Calvin a few vulgar names. Otey balled his fist and made a move to come around the desk.

"Young man, you really don't want to do that," Calvin recited some verses reminding him that the battle was not with the young man in front of him but with the demon that chose to use the boy as a vessel to do Satan's bidding.

Otey came around the desk and got in Calvin's face. "Yeah I do."

"I bet you won't hit'em." Calvin was surprised to hear Omarion declare.

"Yeah Otey, hit him," Charlie egged him on.

"Emily—I" Calvin tried to call for help, hoping the student would get up and go to the office. Instead, Emily didn't budge but the look on her face showed her horror and disbelief. Calvin saw one of the Hispanic students slip out to the back and prayed to God that the student was going to get help.

"Emily, you get up and I'm going to knock him down." Charlie threatened. A wicked grin formed on her face. "Swing on him," Charlie demanded.

"Yeah, knock Mr. Rice Cake out," another student declared.

Calvin sized up Otey. They were equal in height and in build. Calvin had eight years on the young man, but Otey played basketball and Calvin was sure the boy worked out more than he did. And he knew Otey was good with the hands because he'd broken up a fight the boy gotten into earlier in the semester.

I need my job, Calvin reminded himself, *I can't swing on this boy even if he does manage to hit me.*

Calvin picked up the phone and dialed the two digit code for an administrator to come to the class room. Otey knocked the phone out of his hand and took a swing on Calvin, barely missing his lip.

"I oughta be able to stream music, play computer games or do whatever I want." Otey demand as he moved around like a boxer—waiting for the next opportunity to swing again.

"Otey, I'm going to request one more time that you go back to your seat."

"Man, I ain't going nowhere. I paid my ten dollars and if I can't do what I please then I need to get my money back."

Otey pushed Calvin and Calvin almost fell into the corner. He'd thought about escaping but he didn't want to take a chance on the fact that Otey would accidentally cause more ruckas—hitting another student and causing an even bigger fight. Calvin blocked the blow that was meant for his face and quickly countered by blocking another body blow and stepping to the right side.

Calvin didn't restrain the young man because doing so would make him seem like the aggressor—even though it was his word versus the students. Calvin also knew that without a camera, the students could gang up and create any story they wanted.

Wes stepped in the room and quickly got behind Otey and restrained him—removing him from the classroom. Some of the students were disappointed that Otey didn't get to beat up on Calvin.

"Write Otey up and any student involved in encouraging him."

Calvin nodded his head. Chante, Charlie, Omarion to name a few. Technically, he'd have to write up the whole class with the exception of the physically disabled students, the non-English speaking Hispanics, Emily and Austin.

With Otey out of the room, Calvin looked at the students—many whom were still laughing. "Everyone have a seat—now." Calvin snapped. He was two seconds from forgetting his salvation and going off on everyone.

Calvin watched as most of the students complied with his request. "Charlie—you take Chante and Omarion and go with him."

"But—" Omarion barely got the word out before Calvin interrupted him.

"Y'all wanted me to get knocked out? Well this is what knocked out feels like. Starting at this moment, I'm suspending computer privileges for everyone. We are going to do this unit with just pen, paper and packets until I feel like this class has earned the right to participate in a lab. If you don't like it—there's the door. I won't stop you, but be man or woman enough to deal with the consequences."

Calvin opened the closed door, stepped aside and invited anyone who wanted to leave to bounce.

No one got up.

Mr. Rice's Classroom – Butler J. Parker High
2:42 PM

"I can't believe that I spent all the time writing up all the students who were involved in the incident and described in detail what their involvement was. And all a few of them got was one day of after school detention."

Miguel and Reverend Conseco shook their heads as they watched Calvin set up for the FBLA meeting.

"At my old school—they may have been low performing and below standards in many areas academically and otherwise, but a student never got away with threatening or carrying out physical harm against any adult."

"I understand your frustration Calvin, really I do." Reverend Conseco said, "all you can do is document that this happened and pray that it doesn't happen again."

Calvin shook his head.

"Mr. Rice," Charlie waited at the door.

Calvin shook his head—he definitely did not want Charlie to be part of any organization or event he was putting together. The child was nothing but trouble and he knew that her involvement would lead to nothing but that.

"Come and have a seat," Miguel invited Charlie in to his dismay.

They watched as Charlie quietly took a seat near the front— unusual for her. Another few students who weren't in any of his classes came in as well. He recognized a few from being on the hall and prayed that the students have taken the business classes offered at the school. Anyone was welcomed, but to have a shot at winning any of the contests, being able to grasp the concepts taught in the CTE courses was a must.

At 2:47, Calvin started the interest meeting with just six students. At the school Calvin had done some of his student teaching at, their chapter had about thirty members with twenty two to twenty-five being active at any given meeting. Five of those members were also members of the school's DECA chapter. At that school, the FBLA chapter and the DECA chapter did some joint events and some of the same community service projects. At most schools, the DECA and FBLA chapters may have joint members, but they do not do projects together.

Calvin had invited DECA members to join and even stayed after for their last meeting to personally extend the invitation—not one member of the marketing organization showed up.

"So when do I get to be president?" Charlie asked after Calvin presented the organization's history.

"We have to have a vote and active participation. Everyone here would have to register, pay dues and we can go from there."

Charlie walked up to Calvin, pulled out a stack of money, gave Calvin two Benjamins. "This ought to cover dues for everyone here. Can I be president now so I can show y'all how it works?"

"Charlie, you can't buy your way into office," Calvin stressed.

"If I want it, I buy it. Now unless you can get anyone who would vote me out—"

Calvin decided it wasn't worth arguing about. In the back of his mind, he knew he'd have to try to find students who weren't scared of Charlie, but he also knew that many of the students were scared of her.

After going over the rest of the information he had, he handed out the applications, refunded Charlie's money so that she could turn it in with a completed application.

"You handled that well," Miguel pointed out after the last of the students were leaving.

"How's Charlie going to be president of FBLA? She barely pays attention in class and keeps up drama. What do I look like?"

"A teacher who's willing to take a vested interest in turning a wayward student into a productive citizen—I see an opportunity," Miguel said.

"An opportunity?"

"Yes—an opportunity. We must believe that as teachers—we are the gatekeepers and keys to redirecting and encouraging any student to making a life changing decisions. We have to give those whom are undeserving chances so that they may remember these lessons and help us turn others around with their time comes."

"I never thought of it that way," Calvin confessed.

"I heard about what Otey and some of the other students did to you—and I know it seems unfair that we are held to a higher standard than they are—but you have to always remember that you are charged to take the higher ground. That is what being an educator is all about."

"You're right."

"I tell you what, why don't you come to my church in three weeks? It's a small, multi-racial church that I believe you will enjoy."

"Okay, I think I can do three weeks. My brother will be out of jail by then so maybe he can join us."

Miguel put his hand on Calvin's shoulder, "remember all is not lost—keep the faith."

Calvin was determined to do that as he looked at his schedule to see when he could fit in another FBLA meeting within the next two weeks. He was going to need all the faith he could muster if Charlie was going to lead the organization this year.

Chapter Twenty

Calvin couldn't believe that he had done a parent-teacher via Skype in his classroom. Getting some of the parents to cooperate had been hassle—so he didn't mind making the accommodation and working with a parent who was trying to work with their child. He hated doing some of phone conferences. Some of the parents or the guardian of the student involved would be rude. They would call him every name but a child of God and expect him to eat it up because he was on one side of the phone and they were on the other.

If only they knew that he was *this* close to backsliding—*this* close to backhanding one of them if he'd ever saw them in person. But that line of thinking was in conflict with the man he desired to be.

When the call finally ended, he looked at the time on his monitor and saw that he still was stuck in the classroom for another hour. He couldn't loosen the rosemary and silver-colored tie or unbutton the salmon colored shirt so that he could breathe. Calvin really wanted to call up Mrs. Vargas and see if she'd offer some information on where Maria was. It had been two weeks and Calvin still hadn't found her. Any other time, the woman would be calling him and getting on his everlasting nerve. But when Maria disappeared so did Mrs. Vargas and Calvin was starting to enjoy that.

Calvin pulled up the online radio station and turned it to the Latin station and the soothing sounds of tango filled his workspace. He grabbed the stack of worksheets that he had started grading during his break but quickly got board. He lazily looked through the school email and decided that there were no memos that needed his urgent attention.

Calvin pulled out his Toshiba laptop and soon, he was working on another graduate assignment. He'd been slacking on his graduate studies and didn't want to fail. He was only three credits away from clearing his lateral entry license and halfway through his master's program.

Just as he was getting ready to get into the assignment, he saw Evelyn standing at the door. "Mr. Rice, are you busy?"

"No—come on in."

Calvin put the stack of papers he was grading back on the pile he was working on. He knew that she was coming to talk about the evaluation. He got up from his desk and offered to meet her at the computers.

"I came to talk about your evaluation. I wanted to catch you before you went to Greensboro—you are going to Greensboro?"

"Yes, I'm going for one of my classes," Calvin fell into his private conversation as if he were talking to one of his boys as opposed to an administrator he barely could stand to be around.

"I wish you the best on that," Evelyn said as she ruffled through some papers. She pulled out two copies of the evaluation form that she had filled out. "I'm not going to lie, it took me a few years before I got my masters. But now that I have it, the sky is the limit. I've been debating whether or not I should go for my doctorate."

Calvin nodded his head yes. He could care less what Evelyn did with her degree or her life. He didn't trust her further than he could see he but he knew that remaining cordial was the Christian thing to do.

"You know you sound stressed—let me guess—another parent-teacher conference?" Evelyn seemed concerned.

"I sound *that* bad?" Calvin hoped he didn't sound like he wasn't interested in the parents.

"One thing twenty years of education has taught me was to recognize a teacher in distress."

Calvin looked up. He didn't think the worry he had for Maria was that visible. He'd talked to Miguel and Reverend Conseco and knew that his conversation about Maria didn't go beyond those two.

"I'm sure with all of the school and work, it's starting to wear on you. Aren't you going to the Diamond and Pearls Ball in a couple of weeks? Wes has been talking about it and indiscreetly trying to raise money for the scholarships. I'm thinking about making an appearance there myself."

"You?" Calvin was shocked. There was no way he could picture the stiff-neck administrator letting loose at a ball that would be attended by professionals only twenty years her junior.

"Yes me," Evelyn sounded offended. "Don't think that because I'm old that I still don't know how to cut a rug. If I remember correctly, it was my generation that created the electric slide, soul music and the foundation of rap music. Not to mention that my sorority is cohosting."

"You're right," Calvin conceded.

"Of course I'm right. Why don't you go to the ball?"

"I'm going," Calvin started to reveal more but stopped.

"I came to bring you the evaluation. This not a bad report but there are some highlights that I want to go over with you before this goes into your file."

"Thank you," Calvin took the report and glanced through it.

"First I want to point out some of your strengths. You are very clear and concise with your instruction and you are very good at using the Smart Board to interact with the class."

"Thank you. I finally feel like I finally got the hang of the Smart Board." Calvin commented. "The training I had last week helped out a whole lot."

"Also, you are very knowledgeable about the concepts and presenting real-life concepts to the class. That is very important to make sure that the students know how the education they are learning in this class applies to the real world."

Calvin nodded his head. He remembered the presentations he'd done at Winston-Salem State and at A&T and how his professors used the devices in the class. Also, the mock teaching lessons and simulations were starting to pay off as well.

"The areas I'd like to see you improve on are addressing inappropriate behavior the moment it happens. Like, a few minutes after one of the senior students had finished their assignment—ole girl nodded off in class."

"I caught her," Calvin defended.

"Yes, but still the fact that she was able to move the objects out of her way and make room to lay her head down at the computers—if I were a county evaluator, that would have been a major problem.

"Also, some of the students finish the assignments very fast and are left with ample amount of time to get into mischievous behavior."

"That I admit I need to work on. I don't want to create filler assignments just to have them do something to keep them busy—but I've had some level of difficulty finding projects that I could easily use because what I see is that the students in my class are friends with students who had Mrs. Fieldtag last semester."

Calvin noticed Evelyn nodding her head. "And they already had the assignments because the curriculum hasn't changed much since last year."

"This is what I'd like to suggest. I want you to change the way you incorporate some of the media in your classroom. Maybe start the day with a video—a news article—some current event that will require the students to research. I know that in your curriculum you will be doing job applications so maybe have them bring in a job application from work on a day. This will keep them on their toes and keep them from guessing what you are going to do next.

"Then go to your Essential Question and focus on the most important theme you want for them to get out of the classroom for the day.

"Then incorporate the lesson and the assignment given them the example—and once that is done, give them enough time to get it done. During that time, if you are going to work with Omarion on his reading—which you shouldn't because that is not your responsibility, you work with him then—especially since he has modified assignments.

"After they have the allotted time, use the last five minutes to do daily pop quizzes—allow Omarion that time to read. Perhaps reward the multiple students who want to help him would be some external contest you create. Or maybe at the end of the day instead of you doing the recap on what would work—you select two or three students and have them do the end of the day recap so that you can take note on who's listening and whose not. Those who've been caught not being on point can be put on the spot the next day."

Calvin thought about it and admitted that Evelyn had a good idea. He had always wanted to incorporate more technology but had no idea how to do it. He looked over the written evaluation and was determined to become a better teacher and work harder to make sure that he was more on point.

Chapter Twenty-One

Saturday, October 25, 2008
Rice Residence
2:45 PM

Calvin woke up mad and Madea was right, he was not over it yet because he still wanted to kick Bilal's butt. Last night, he had cried himself to sleep. His wife was putting a hurting on him that he was in no way prepared to deal with. In fact, he could not remember any other time in his life where he had ever hurt as bad. When a man loved someone the way that he loved his wife, he's willing to do anything it takes to keep her, no matter what it may cost him in the end. At first he thought money was the reason Maria cheated, so he considered applying for a part time job at a grocery store just so he could have enough money to pay *their* bills; as well as a little extra for Maria to play with.

He ignored his ringing doorbell—something he become accustomed to doing since Maria left. Calvin desperately tried to avoid his mother or anyone else who had something negative to say about his situation. He preferred to sit around the house and listen to Mary J. Blige. She seemed to be the only one who could identify with his problems.

After twenty four hours of Mary and her life, sharing her world and trying to get the drama out of his life, Calvin got up and looked through his CD rack and finally decided to put in Toni Braxton's latest CD. She got it right on the first track when she reminded him that he had to breathe and move on with his life. The doorbell rang again and he could hear a set of keys jiggling and trying to fit into the door knob. He knew he couldn't ignore it and hoped that maybe Maria had come to her senses and realized that their marriage wasn't over, and that they could save it. The minute he thought about the fact that he was naked, excited and he realized that she could see him through the window. At first he thought he should get some pants on, but then he decided that maybe some spontaneous loving was exactly what their marriage needed. Maybe the answer to their marital problems lied between his legs.

"I've been trying to get at you for a few days?" Martin walked in and gave him a hug. To say that Calvin was disappointed to see his best friend was an understatement given his present condition. After all these years, he couldn't believe that his boy looked so much like Tyrese. Martin wore a muscle shirt that allowed the world to see his "Ain't No Punk Christian" tattoo on his right bicep.

"Let me get decent," Calvin was defeated. He had almost forgotten that he had given Martin a set of keys to assure his mother and father that he would be safe in Winston-Salem. It's been almost four years since they graduated from college and he had never asked his best friend to return the key back to him.

"What's good?" Toni Braxton sang through the stereo, moving the album along.

Martin shook his head as he picked up a current issue of *Black Enterprise* from the coffee table. Martin was a little ticked that Calvin had been rude and not invited him in or at least warned him that he was baby boy fresh.

"Have you packed to go to the airport tomorrow?" Martin asked when Calvin returned to the living room. Calvin looked at him, shook his head to indicate that he hadn't and took a seat on the couch. "So I take it you aren't trying to go to the ball your frat is having with the AKAs' tonight either?"

Calvin had been so depressed in his funk that he forgot about the Diamonds & Pearls Ball which his alumni chapter and the local AKA alumni chapter used to raise money for academic scholarships they give to students attending HBCU's. Calvin got to thinking about how long it's been since he been to a fraternity function.

"I'm surprised you're not dressed in your black and gold," Calvin replied. "I haven't been thinking right since Maria left, man."

"Look man, you can deal with Maria and the divorce later," Martin back tracked when he thought how cold his words were. "You can't let a woman who doesn't appreciate you bring you down. I mean, I haven't been through a divorce but you can't let the divorce consume your life." He noticed the foul odor coming from his friend. Martin was not used to seeing his friend down in the dumps like this.

"Let's get you ready to go," Martin encouraged him. "You go take a shower while I find you something to wear."

"But what about my hair? I need a shape up," Calvin came to the reality of how unkempt his appearance was.

"Calvin, when have you *ever* walked out of this house looking a mess?" A reminiscent smile spread across Martin's face. "I remember when you were Mr. Ram, you had a new hairstyle every three or four days it seemed like and you always had something fly to wear."

It was true. Calvin remembered those days fondly. Even though he was a newlywed and getting ready for the birth of his son, he still felt the need to keep sexy coming back. Calvin walked up the stairs to the bedroom, stepped into the bathroom and turned on the water. Calvin looked at himself in the mirror—he looked and felt a mess. He could hear Toni singing about how he was so stupid and he had to agree with her.

Calvin reached for the Nubian Heritage Indian Hemp & Haitian Vetiver soap and inhaled the smell as a means to calm his body. He allowed the light bristles to attempt to scrub away the pain of his divorce. The fragrance smelled so good and he felt like falling asleep right there but he couldn't. He breathed and exhaled and felt the weight of all his drama and stress roll off his back and fall in the tub. If only he could see it going down the drain. He scrubbed away, washing off Maria and Bilal and every mean and evil thing that has happened in the past two years.

Calvin grabbed his robe and put it on over his undergarments. He brushed his teeth and rinsed, humming along with the songs as the CD played. He walked to the room and sat on the bed and put on the same scented lotion as the soap that he had scrubbed with in the shower. His allergies to regular perfumes and fragrances were so severe that over the years he had probably become the most faithful consumer Nubian Heritage ever had. He looked over to the left and noticed that Martin found the white and crème Armani suit that he thought he got rid of after he and Maria got married. Calvin really didn't want to wear it at first but once he put the suit on, he was surprised that he still looked good in it after putting on a few extra pounds.

"Yo!" Calvin was excited. "I still got it."

Martin had the look of the proud father when he saw Calvin admiring himself in the mirror. Now he remembered why Maria bought the suit. He smiled and started dancing to the music.

"This is what I needed," Calvin admitted.

"And we are going to make sure you stay *needed*. You look really good."

"Thank you."

"Pull out those diamond cufflinks and my crushed red diamond tie, they go good with this suit."

Martin did as he was told. He also came back with some hair clippers. Calvin took the suit jacket off and Martin got to work giving Calvin a much needed shape up. He wished he had thought to do that before Calvin got in the shower but it would be alright. Martin was just happy to see his friend smiling again. Calvin changed undershirts and went to the bathroom to dampen a towel so he could go over his hairline. Once he completed that task and put his shirts back on, Calvin was ready to go. When Martin came back into the room, he wore a dark crème suit with matching shoes with a black shirt and gold tie.

"If I didn't know any better, I'd think you were trying to outshine me."

"I got to do my best," Martin remarked. "I am single and I need to find a nice Christian girl I can bring home to mama."

"And you think you are going to meet her at the ball?"

Martin looked him over, "with the way you are dressed, I should be asking you the same thing."

Calvin punched Martin in the arm and they went about play sparring, as if they were kids again. When Martin landed a blow to the chest, they both knew it was time to stop.

"For real, I'm not looking for another woman, but if I do find one, it'll make it easier to forget my whole situation."

Martin nodded his head and the gentlemen left the house. Calvin deeply inhaled the air and when he exhaled, the thoughts of his pending sin in granting Maria's request for a divorce slipped his mind.

Martin's Crib
6:45 PM

"Yo' Calvin," Martin flossed in the rented black stretch Hummer that he and Calvin chipped in to use for the evening, "you mind if I put this new Mary Mary on? I'm feeling this new 'God in Me' song they got on this album.

Calvin smiled when he heard the Auto-Tune over the synthesizers that were used from the track. The song sounded like one of the songs the popular rappers his students listened to on the radio or on their iPods. "Word? Put that on."

The bass in the song along with the way Erica and Tina confidently reminded everyone that it was God who provided all of their blessings kept Calvin's head nodding. Calvin caught a glimpse of himself in the rearview mirror and was happy that he stepped out of his funk and agreed to go to the Diamonds and Pearls Ball. It was one of the biggest social events of the year and all the elite black folks in the Piedmont Triad were going to be in attendance.

"So why are we picking these women up again?" Calvin brought up the subject of Martin trying to pre-arrange a blind date for him.

"Man, you gotta stop being so uptight and just appreciate the fact that someone's looking out for you." Martin was irritated that Calvin would ruin the mood of the song. "I know you're *still* married and I'm not telling you to sleep with the girl. I'm telling you to engage her, entertain her and be open to the idea that you guys can have Christian fun together."

Martin had driven the Hummer from his condo to the Marriott hotel in downtown Winston-Salem. "These women came all of the way from Raleigh to support the event so I need for you to behave and so them how a Denver boy gets down."

Within minutes of bringing the Hummer to a complete stop, Martin quickly got out of the car and went to escort four, fine young women into the backseat of the ride. For a moment, Calvin felt like one of those scrubs Chili was singing about even though he was paying for the ride. Of the four, one woman caught his attention wearing a Mary and Miriam evening gown that accentuated the curves on her chest and her hips in all the right places on her five foot eight frame. She carried herself with the same style and grace that the singer, Monica had and that turned Calvin on.

"Good evening," Calvin greeted as he moved over and offered the ladies the seats near the doors.

"Good evening to you as well. I'm Keisha?" the woman who caught his eye said. Being the gentlemen, Calvin replied by giving her his name and taking her hand and kissing it. When he looked into her eyes, he knew that under different circumstances, Keisha had the ability to be his trophy wife. If he weren't married, he'd work hard to make that a reality.

"You look really beautiful." Calvin looked around and he engaged each of the other ladies who entered the Hummer. "As do the rest of you."

"And you look handsome yourself," Keisha replied as she reached up and gave Calvin a kiss on the cheek. As Keisha took to her seat comfortably, Calvin put on his seatbelt and Martin proceeded to drive them to their destination.

Calvin listened to the ladies talk about some of the women in their sorority that they had not seen in a while and couldn't help but feeling conflicted and disturbed. The way his heart fluttered, the perspiration that started to form and the way the blood seemed to add extra weight to his midsection were all signs of lust and he hated that he had committed adultery in his heart. He had been so mad and angry at how Maria just up and left with Bilal and here he was, in no better position thinking about all the things he would do with Keisha if he weren't saved. Even the thought of negotiating his sin for repentance had him thinking even more twisted thoughts that were starting to pull him away from Jesus.

Calvin prayed and pleaded with his flesh to be still and not make his presence known. The last thing he wanted was for the ladies to think they were sitting with a perv and to be ducking and dodging him for the rest of the night. Calvin noticed the way

Keisha would steal glances in his direction—a wink here and a smile there. *She probably thinks I'm a chump.* Calvin thought to himself while trying to keep his composure. He envisioned all of the freaky things he was looking to do with her and just knew he couldn't do like Luther Vandross and have her for just one night. Just because Maria cheated on him doesn't mean that he was going to cheat on her back.

"Why are you so quiet?" Keisha called him out. She reminded him of Lisa, one of the girls he grew up with in Denver that he had a slight crush on growing up.

"I got a lot on my mind," Calvin confessed, "but one thing I do know is that I want to have a good time."

"We will," Keisha moved closer to him. She grabbed his hands and it appeared natural for their fingers to interlock.

"Wow!" Calvin felt like a nerd who had touched a girl for the very first time.

"I didn't know you were shy," Keisha blew up his spot.

"Trust me, I'm usually not. It's just something about being with you that has me tongue tied," Calvin couldn't believe his player card was slipping from his fingers. Having played his weak hand already, he flashed his million dollar smile, knowing that he'd impress her as he'd impressed hundreds of ladies before.

The other three women talked among themselves while Calvin and Keisha continued their own private conversation. Calvin liked the way Keisha's hand felt inside of his and was surprised that he felt normal holding her hand. He expected to feel conviction for being *this* close to a woman who wasn't his wife but he didn't. After riding for another mile, they pulled up to the Anderson Center on the campus of Winston-Salem State University where the invitation-only gala was taking place. Martin pulled up to the entrance and soon, was letting Calvin and the ladies out of the Hummer. As Calvin held his arm out for

Keisha to slip into, he asked her, "when was the last time you been to a dance?"

"About two years ago. I didn't make it to my church's formal ball that they had last year."

"Well tonight, I promise you that we are going to have a good time." Calvin was determined to make up from his sudden onset of shyness.

Anderson Center, Winston-Salem State University

7:08 PM

Maria walked into the ballroom at the Anderson Center and she was amazed at how the place was decorated for the night's event. Knowing that her husband's fraternity was co-sponsoring the event, she almost didn't show up but she knew she wouldn't miss one of the largest social events in the city. She was still Calvin's wife and didn't see a problem with attending. For the last few days, in her guilt, she'd knock on the door. Maria hoped that Calvin would come out of the condo and each time she knock or she saw other people drop by to check on him, Calvin was nonresponsive.

Once inside, the chandelier was bright and almost blinding as Maria saw little crystals falling from the frame like raindrops. The crimson and crème decorations made her feel like she had stepped inside of a castle and the faux diamonds and pearls that not only seemed to grow from the ground but were strategically draped from many of the statues.

Maria almost wished that Bilal had come with her. In fact, she asked him but he responded that not only did he not feel comfortable going to an event that was affiliated with the fraternity that Calvin was a part of, but he also didn't support their causes because he thought being a member of the group was in conflict with God's will.

"Maria," she turned around at the calling of her name and she was surprised to see Calvin standing behind her with another woman on his arms. Maria felt her heart jump to her throat and she wanted to croak. Adding insult to injury, Keisha was rocking style of the same dress except hers was an ivory color that she had gotten from Nordstrom's in Charlotte a few days earlier. And she saw the bald headed man that she thought looked like Mr. Clean and when he turned around, she quickly identified Martin. She should've known he wasn't going to be too far behind.

"I didn't know you were going to be here?" Maria stated, struggling with her words. She looked down at her ring finger and noticed she didn't have it on. She glanced at his and was shocked that not only was he wearing his, but that Keisha didn't seem to mind.

"You must be Maria," Keisha stepped forward in an effort to shake a hand that was not extended to her. "I'm Keisha."

"You moved on pretty fast?" Maria questioned as she rolled her eyes at Keisha and redirected her focus back to Calvin, who seemed amused by all of this.

"I don't move as fast as you," Calvin countered. "Keisha and I aren't dating so you can peel your scales back. Keisha and her girls have come all the way from Raleigh to support our event and I promised Martin that I'd take care of his guest."

Maria didn't want to go on the defensive. She was the one who messed things up by sleeping around with Bilal but she couldn't deny that Calvin was spectacular and fancy as Drake would say and she wished she were the one on his arm. She already knew that she had played herself out to be a whore in every sense of the word and if anything, Keisha would prove to be a formidable opponent should she try to make a move to get Calvin back.

"Well, I hope you enjoy the event," Maria tried to reply with the least amount of venom as possible. The fact that Keisha and her girls were wearing the same pearl earrings with the small pink studs around them let Maria know that the ladies were tighter than tight. All of a sudden, she didn't feel like she belonged and began to search for an exit.

Earth Wind and Fire's "Let's Grove" brought some of the old heads and rising stars to the dance floor and Maria watched as Calvin and Keisha made their way to the crowd. Maria admired the way Calvin's body moved as he kept in step with Keisha. For that moment in time, she regretted moving things with Bilal the way she had and wished she could get Calvin to one of the small meeting rooms and that they could move like that in private. Not too far away from them, Martin was dancing with one of the girls that he'd come into the dance with and pretty soon, she didn't see any of them at all as more and more people made their way to the dance floor. Surprisingly, the DJ kept the pace with Montell Jordan's "This is How We Do It." At that moment, Maria spotted the young white girl who was giving the older, Dick Van Dyke-look-a-like a run for his money.

Maria looked into the crowd. The young girl following a man who was old enough to be her grandfather away from the dance floor caught her attention. She watched as they headed toward one of the elevators that surely led to his room for the night. Her guilt grew about what she had done. In a distance, she observed Calvin and Keisha enjoying a drink and some hors d'oeuvres. She wished Keisha the best of luck—in the back of her mind. Just as she was turning to leave, she saw an older woman who she remembered had a daughter around her age. Maria remembered how mean-spirited and nasty the woman seemed to be every time she would be around her. Funny how karma came back around. The woman was loaded with alcohol and money and Maria could tell just by the way she raised her voice that she was either at or near her alcohol capacity. And that was the perfect recipe to get the information she needed to get the revenge she always wanted to have.

***

Calvin and Martin walked into the ballroom and were greeted by a fabulous and thick sista interpreting "And I Am Telling You I'm Not Going." Calvin began to miss Maria and the way she used to sing to him when they first got married. That was his favorite song to hear her sing because of the way her beautiful voice carried the song. When she sang that song—when she sang *any* song, Calvin felt like he was the only man in her world.

When she was done, the mood changed as Usher's voice began to pump from the speakers massive speakers that lined the edge of the stage. He was telling the ladies that they didn't have to call. Calvin was thinking the same thing as the upbeat tempo got him hype. The new initiates of Calvin's fraternity were rocking suits with vests or nice button ups and slacks in their fraternity's colors and began strolling on the dance floor. Calvin joined in with some of the alumni members who knew the stroll. He felt good being amongst his brothers and began to remember his days as an active member of the collegiate chapter. When they were finished and the DJ switched the song to another selection, Calvin spotted Martin sitting at the table talking to two women of another sorority.

"Calvin, this is Kima and Pam." Calvin shook their hands and sat in the empty seat next to Kima. "Vincent went to go bring back some drinks for the ladies while his lady, Pam, went to go freshen up," Martin announced to Calvin.

"Vincent—as in Minister Farrakhan Vincent?"

Kima and Pam chuckled at the disappointed look that Martin gave Calvin.

"That is foul and un-Christ like Calvin. We're supposed to treat others as we'd want to be treated."

"That's right, it is un-Christ like," Kima tried to agree but couldn't stop the chuckling.

"All Muslims are not Minister Farrakhan Calvin," Keisha appeared to be genuinely offended by the comment. Calvin was confused because a few seconds ago, she was laughing with her girl.

"Please be nice to Vincent," Martin was serious and began nursing the glass of water he was cradling, "I can't have my best friend and my line brother fighting at this function. Sorors will never let me hear the end of it."

"Um-um—naw, we not trying to have that," Kima seconded as she began to take an interest in Calvin. She was trying to figure out the fragrance he was wearing but she couldn't place her name on it. She knew it wasn't cologne but whatever it was, it smelled good on him. She was sizing him up and he passed the inspection until she noticed the wedding band on his left finger. "How long have you been married?"

Calvin looked at her dumbfounded. He hadn't told her that he was married but took the hint when she gave a subtle reference to his hand. He looked down on his reminder of his vows and his promise before the Lord to honor and to love his wife until death did him part. He was sad because one thing Calvin tried to do was avoid lying to God. He know that God could see everything and hear everything, even the whispers of his heart but he felt that he was letting God down by allowing Maria to leave him and finally excepting that she was gone. It still wasn't easy. It hadn't been that long since she left, but he knew that he had to let go.

"I'm in the process of getting a divorce," Calvin finally verbally acknowledged the transition of his life. He took the ring off and put it in his pocket. "I've been so used to wearing this thing every day because it meant so much to me, but I'm finding that the ring doesn't mean the same thing to everyone. My wife left me a few days ago."

"I'm sorry, I didn't know," Kima apologized but the damage had been done.

"No." Calvin paused, "I need to accept that this is where I am at with my life and move on and maybe meet the woman God intends for me to spend the rest of my life with."

Calvin stared at the imprint of his wedding ring and realized it was the first time he had taken it off in a few days. He often left it on when he showered so moments were few and far between when the ring was parted from him. He was beginning to regret being so adamant against getting a prenuptial agreement as he thought about not only of his wife cheating on him with another man, but them enjoying half of everything, even if it wasn't much, that he had spent his entire life since graduation to build. Marriage, like an initiation in a membership of a black Greek letter fraternity, was supposed to be a life time commitment; a prenuptial should not have been necessary.

"Well if you need space, I can give you that."

An uneasy discomfort came over Calvin's eyes as Vincent's arrived to help Pam sit in her seat across from him. Vincent equally displeased to see Calvin as well.

"Nice to meet you Pam," Calvin extended his hand to greet hers and she smiled. He tried to remember where knew three other women named Keisha, Kima and Pam but couldn't see it. No one else came to mind so he decided to enjoy their company. "I don't need anymore space," he replied to Kima's offer. "I'm gonna be fine."

"Well that's good."

"Now that we got that out the way," Martin popped open a bottle of sparkling grape juice that had been on ice in the middle of the table. "I say you get to know her," Martin pointed at Calvin and Kima. "I'll get to know her," he referred to Keisha as he poured some of the juice in their glasses and acknowledged Vincent and Pam. "And ya'll do what ya'll do."

***

Saturday, October 25, 2008
Rice Residence
8:45 AM

Martin probably should have been more specific when he said "get to know her." Martin and Keisha made plans to leave the party and to go sight-seeing; just the two of them. Vincent and Calvin were never going to be much for a conversation, so he and Pam dipped on them shortly after Martin and Keisha left. As for Calvin and Kima, the drinks led them to the dance floor, along with some of the other people who came to the Diamonds and Pearls Ball. After they danced they went to TGI Fridays where they had a nice meal and mingled with some of the other people from the ball who ended up there afterwards as well.

When dinner ended Calvin and Kima were both a little tipsy, yet Calvin took the risk and drove Kima back to his place. It was after one o'clock in the morning and yet he felt guilty because he almost expected his wife to be home. When he didn't see her car, Calvin felt safe and he let Kima inside.

***

Only a few minutes earlier, he had been struggling to write a message for the next youth meeting. A message that it didn't look like he was going to be able to write, or even be able to attend the next youth meeting.

He could feel the breeze on his legs letting him know that he had left the window open. He looked over to the see that the maroon curtains were closed but flew into the room just a little bit. He started to reach out to close the window when he was brought back to the reason why he couldn't concentrate on the paper he was supposed to be working on. He was trapped in his seat by a pair of arms that had reached out to grab his chair. His legs were shaking and his eyes were rolled back as he looked down at the bald, caramel head that was bouncing up and down on his midsection. He was scared that it might have been a man that he was with until he smelled the familiar scent of a woman and he relaxed knowing that he was cool. As he grabbed her head with his left hand, he looked to his right to see his pants were laying across the floor and his dress shirt hanging on the stair railing. The woman with the caramel head was not supposed to be pleasing him like this—especially since he'd just come to grips with the idea of getting a divorce, He was, after-all, the one teaching teens how to abstain from sex in the church. She had his lips on Calvin's precious jewels with his legs over her shoulders, rendering him helpless.

It dawned on Calvin that he and Maria had not sex in weeks. It was not celibacy by choice, either Calvin was too tired or Maria came home too late to give him any, but today he had given in to that temptation in lustful sin. Now not only was he getting a divorce, he was committing adultery. Trust, it wasn't planned. He hadn't even been thinking about sex. Calvin was the kind of guy that avoided all of the bars and clubs he used to hang out at when he was single. He had avoided some of the ex-girlfriends that he used to give a little piece of himself to. When Calvin got saved and agreed to help with the youth ministry, he wanted to be a role model, an inspiration, and a goal for what a man had to look forward to when they saved themselves for marriage, but he could relate to those who found it hard not to give into temptation.

As he threw Kima on the couch and got on top of her naked body, he reached behind the cushions for his stash of massage oils. Like **R**. Kelly, he was feeling on her booty while trying to feel around for the oil and some rubbers that he now realized that he had thrown away. With this realization, he stopped—he stopped touching her completely, and he moved her legs so he could sit on the couch. Calvin looked at the hair on his chest and the happy trail that led to between his legs.

He wanted to do her right.

Then he looked ahead and saw the picture of Jesus hanging on the wall. He saw his colored body hanging on the cross for his sins and Kima's. As the she put her lips at the tip of his sword, Calvin brought her head up and shook his head. He looked at her body and had admit, she had nice shape and probably went to the gym more than he did. .

"Yo, what's up, I thought we were going to get down?" Kima asked and Calvin could see the disappointment on her face.

"Nah, I can't do it," Calvin was happy that his penis finally decided to agree with his thinking brain and go limp. "Just because my wife cheated on me in our bed doesn't make it right for me to do the same to her." Calvin turned to face Kima and lifted her chin up. He could see tears beginning to form in her eyes.

"I'm sorry but I can't have sex with you now," Calvin finally got the strength to say. He knew that Jesus was pleased that he was standing up and doing the right thing—but his flesh was pissed off. It wanted to be fed. "I want to and you are a pretty lady but right now, I'd only let God down and hurt you in the process."

Calvin sounded nice trying to let Kima go gently, but on the inside, he wanted to slap his own face because he was getting ready to let a nice looking woman go. Calvin really wanted to take Kima and let out the frustration of not being able to know his wife's body for a few weeks. He wanted to use Kima to fill the void—get to know her very well.

He knew that would have been wrong.

Calvin expected her to jump up and go crazy on him because he got a little sexual healing and didn't give her any, but she surprised him.

"We cool," Kima said while touching his chest. Calvin was trying to remember how they had gotten to his house to begin with. It certainly wasn't to have sex, it was for something else. Then Calvin remembered that they both were a few glasses short of too much wine and it didn't help that she and Calvin had taken more than a couple shots of liquor while attempting to discuss their problems. While Calvin was going through a divorce, Kima was battling with an abusive ex-fiancé that could not deal with the fact that she looked like a beautiful, light skinned version of India.Aire. She too was now looking at the wall and facing the same picture of Jesus that Calvin was facing. "Sometimes, when I know I'm going to give in, I take the pictures down."

Calvin knew the feeling.

"But don't you feel guilty afterwards though? I mean, He sees and knows everything. Do you repent?"

"It's a part of who I am. My desire for sex does not change how I feel about God," Kima got up and Calvin watched her walk away to the bathroom. Calvin was getting stiff again and the old him would have gotten up and pounced on it. His sword had returned and he sure enough wanted to attack the enemy—stab it a few times until he felt satisfied that he had put it to rest, but he couldn't get the words out of his mouth. Kima turned around and saw him looking at her. Calvin was fixated on the nice plump triangle that was at her midsection. His mouth salivated at that thought of returning the favor of the feeling he had been giving him. Calvin knew he didn't want to go back, for he might not just stop at putting his mouth there. Calvin felt bad that he didn't satisfy her like she had done him, but what was he supposed to do?

He remembered that he hid a condom in one of the cushions. Calvin knew he could put the condom on, handle his business and make sure she was satisfied in the process and let her go but he also knew he couldn't handle that if the roles were reversed.

Calvin still grappled with the idea of actually going through would could be a very nasty divorce. A part of him wanted to soothe the wound of his heart and take a walk on the wild side. Free himself up from his marital commitment and move forward. A part of him wanted to honor God and his vows, for better or for worse.

His body was getting mixed signals and wanted to do its own thing. His body, loved Kima's body and more of what she had to offer.

"Are you changing your mind?" Kima tempted him.

Calvin couldn't think straight. He wanted to be loved and if his wife couldn't love him, this woman was the next best thing.

Calvin got up and she met him halfway and they kissed. She was a great kisser—one of the best Calvin ever had. They took turns jockeying for the dominant space on the wall and like warriors they took their battle to the floor. Calvin grabbed the condom from Kima who picked it up from the floor during their wrestling match, tore the package open as she got on her knees. She backed her mound onto him and rubbing it up and down his shaft. Calvin tapped it twice and then told her to get on her back. He had to admit, it had been a while since he covered his member but like they used to say, it was just like riding a bike. Calvin put her legs up over his shoulders because he always liked looking at Maria when he went inside of her. Just to see the look of surprise and fear in her eyes was enough to turn him on. And just when he was getting the head in good, he looked in her face and all he could see was Maria and he backed away into the wall like he had seen a ghost. Calvin bumped his head against the wall and his heart was racing. Calvin tried rubbing the spot that made contact with the wall to make it feel better but instead, he made it worse.

"It's alright Calvin, we don't have to rush this," Kima got up and walked to the bathroom. As he could hear the shower running, Calvin took the condom off, and at that moment, he thanked God that he wasn't Catholic cause he had no idea how many Hail Mary's he was supposed to say for this. When Kima turned the water off, Calvin quickly asked for forgiveness from God and got up off the floor. Calvin faced her eye to eye as she walked out of the bathroom.

"You alright?"

"Yeah, I am."

"I don't want you to hate me or feel bad about yourself. Everyone gives into a temptation at one point or another. This just happens to be the one we share."

"Yeah," Calvin responded. In the back of his mind, he was criticizing himself for breaking his marital vow. Calvin knew he needed to save himself again for the moment when he could get married to the right woman and eventually make him some babies.

Kima gave him a hug and grabbed her clothes and starting putting them on. Calvin did the same. After making sure that Kima was ready to go, he grabbed the bag he packed earlier as well as an outfit he could change into at the gym, where he decided he would take a shower after he dropped her off. Once they both were ready to go, they walked out the door and into Calvin's car.

Chapter Twenty-Two

Monday, October 27, 2008
Rice's Classroom
10:50 AM

The students were leaving the classroom as Calvin had returned to set up for the upcoming lesson. He had written the following instructions on the board:

1.Go to the sub folders and read the Kanye West Outline and the Kanye West Bio.
2.Read the Outline and the Bio to prepare an unbound report on Kanye West.
3.Use at least three of the sources Calvin provide to help put together the report based on the outline.
4.Follow directions in the Outline for your next assignment.

After getting rid of Kima and resting—he'd taken the time to look at the work the students had submitted for the substitute during the two days he'd been absent. He'd been apprehensive about starting a new lesson with the substitute but the class needed to move on.

"Mr. Rice."

Calvin looked up when Charlie walked in with Sharice not too far in tow.

"Yes," Calvin answered as he watched the two of them take their assigned seats.

"I didn't know you knew about Kanye West."

"He did that song, 'Jesus Walks,'" Calvin decided to humor her.

"He got other songs too," Charlie she started reciting words to one of his popular songs. Calvin flashed a quick smile and then proceeded to make sure that the Smart Board was set up and that he had a sample report available to so that he could give feedback to the students who did good as well as address some problem areas.

After all of the students arrived, Dr. Hewett slipped into the room, which brought smiles on the students faces.

"Mr. Rice," Charlie announced. "I didn't know Dr. Hewett was going to do your observation today."

Calvin thought about her comment and decided not to respond. He knew that she was going to do what she was going to do and he chose to address the issue when the time came.

The expectation was that the students would be quiet during the "Pledge of Allegiance" and may talk quietly during the announcements. He saw how Charlie and Sharice were interacting and decided that he'd walk over there quietly and address them.

"Come on Mr. Rice," Charlie challenged. "We're just gossiping about how Emily almost got beat up at the park the other day."

Emily's face looked like it wanted to hit the floor. She jumped up, "what?"

"Ladies, we are not going to do that in here," Calvin intervened, taking control of the situation. "Everyone, I want to show y'all a sample of the Kanye West report that I wrote based on the seven articles I left for you to research.

As Calvin started his lesson, Austin had gotten up and grabbed the hall pass to go to the restroom. Calvin acknowledged his request and noted Austin was filling out the form.

Calvin started his instruction, pulling a sample report on the screen. Calvin stood and acknowledged the work the students had already begun with the substitute that had been in the room the last two days.

Right when Calvin was getting ready to use his pointer to circle and highlight a passage on the Smart Board, his computer froze.

"I see we are going to have to address this from a different standpoint. Everyone go ahead to the computers and I will send a copy of the corrections to the website and from there, I'll continue the instruction."

Calvin gave time for the students to get to the computers. As they were logging in, Calvin made comments about the papers he had read thus far from the students who attempted to finish the assignment with the substitute last week. Calvin addressed issues and complimented students on what appeared to be right but also acknowledge an error he made in preparing their assignment, leaving off how to put their references together in APA format.

When students attempted to get off task because the computers took longer than normal to load up, Calvin quickly redirected them. "Remember you guys need to sit straight up and not slouch so that you can have good back posture," Calvin pointed out. "We talked about this the first week so that you will decrease the likely hood of developing back problems and other ailments from improper use of the computers."

The students followed directions as requested. Once they were able to pull up the corrections he made to the report, he continued with his lesson. Calvin walked around to individual computers to see what the students had produced thus far.

"Mr. Rice, I have a confession to make," Emily spoke up when he walked past her.

"What is it?" Calvin responded, expecting the worse.

"I've never heard of Kanye West before."

Calvin's eyes blinked so hard, he thought they were going to jump out of its sockets. Even though Calvin didn't listen to much of the rap and R&B that played on the contemporary stations—even he knew who Kanye was. If Kanye wasn't on the cover of magazines, he was popping up on news stations for his controversial remarks.

"Girl, don't sit there and tell that lie," Charlie jumped in.

"Everyone and their mama knows who Kanye West is—and he's right, George Bush does hate black people."

Calvin saw Dr. Hewett's face flush red with embarrassment. Charlie's mouth formed an O and Calvin knew he would catch it for that comment.

"That is his opinion and he's entitled to it." Calvin said.

"Dr. Hewett, do you hate black people?" Austin asked.

A pen dropped and a sheet of paper could be heard sliding across the floor. Everyone's attention turned to Dr. Hewett and the million dollar question. A part of Calvin had always wondered the answer to that question. He was surprised that Austin had the nerve to ask. Equally surprising was the delayed response from Dr. Hewett.

"No, I don't hate black people," Dr. Hewett stated barely above a whisper.

"Everyone needs to get to work now. If you aren't reading the articles I've selected for you—then you need to be creating your own report. Remember to reference the guides on the website." Calvin redirected. Calvin couldn't bring himself to say anything else.

"So back to what I was saying—what do I do about Kanye West?" Emily stated.

"Well—we don't always get to pick the reports we are asked to write about and sometimes, we had to do reports on people or topics we don't like or agree. Prayerfully, that will make our view point stronger. My suggestion is to read all of the articles and then write your report on a common theme found in three or four of the ones you liked the best."

Emily shook her head to indicate that she had understood. Everyone else seemed to be on task except for Otey, whom he'd caught viewing MySpace instead of working on a report or viewing one of the websites. Calvin walked up to Otey and tapped him on the shoulder and asked him to come outside of the classroom. He grabbed one of the detention center passes, quickly wrote Otey's name on it and handed it to him once the boy left the classroom.

MySpace was one of the websites that was supposed to be blocked and not accessed on the servers. Calvin saw Dr. Hewett glaring at him as he stepped back into the classroom.

Near the end of class, Calvin got to get the students together and reviewed what they did in class as a closure. Calvin suspected that many of the students would think they could just sit at the computer, read one or two articles, copy and paste the outline and anticipated and that they would have to do more research to adequately complete the report. Calvin made relevant the purpose of research.

Calvin even used the Obama vs. McCain issue so the students could see that they had to look at the whole reference and read the statement in its entirety. Calvin did address the fact that some of the students wanted to use other sources and Calvin stated why they couldn't use them. Calvin did commend them for wanting to think outside of the box and use other resources that what was documented on the Kanye West Biography. Calvin did not finish the thought when the bell rang.

Calvin saw Dr. Hewett shaking his head as he was walking out of the classroom and knew he would be in the fight of his life to save his job.

Chapter Twenty-Three

Calvin couldn't stand the smell of Polo cologne that emitted heavily from Wes. On him, it smelled like cow manure and myrrh competing for attention and the crap was winning.

Calvin didn't understand why Wes wanted to meet at an eclectic bar. As he had made the walk from his parking space a couple of blocks away, he admired the many murals and other paintings in the heart of Charlotte's art district. Calvin was amazed at the man sitting next to them that had a body full of tattoos that grazed the side of his face to the length of his arm. And based on the tat that began at the base of his neck that led below his waste, he could tell that the man could withstand a lot of pain. Add to the fact that he looked like a snake in the face and his body easily beat out Rick Ross in a hot dog eating contest, Calvin was beyond repulsed.

"I brought you here because we bruhs and I don't want our friendship and bond to change."

"Why would it?" Calvin questioned.

"Dr. Hewett recommended that you be terminated at the end of this semester," Wes got right to the point.

Calvin rolled his eyes. The man in him wanted to punch Wes in his grill and then find Dr. Hewett and deal with him on GP.

"Hey girl," Wes was flirting with some young chick that had made her presence known. Wes slipped into player mode as if he on the prowl. Forgetting that he had his wedding band on or that he just delivered some devastating news to Calvin, Wes continued to fraternize with the chick in his lap, doing some nasty little dance to the beat of the sexual charged R&B song that boomed the radio. "And this is my boy Calvin."

The young woman revealed all of her pearly whites as she looked Calvin's way. He had to admit, the young lady became more attractive by the second and he could see why Wes was digging on her. Unlike sewer breath standing next to her, Calvin could not only smell the Altoids she'd popped into her mouth. He could instantly see that she was the type of chick that wanted a man who was going places.

"Nice to meet you," Calvin offered his hand but she reached for a hug instead, bringing her body extra close to his. Calvin stepped back and allowed himself another good look before taking his seat.

Calvin wanted to finish his conversation with Wes, but he knew that the conversation wouldn't end nowhere near good. Wes was trying too hard to keep the lady at his side when truthfully she was more interested in Calvin to begin with. The lady humored Wes for a few more seconds then handed Calvin her card and told her to call him as she wandered to another man that had caught her eye.

"So what's this about me being terminated?" Calvin got right to the point.

"Dr. Hewett says you don't know how to manage a classroom and that you are unorganized. He's using that and the fact that you are lateral entry status to get rid of you. You need to step your game up."

"Wow—you brought me to a bar to tell me that," Calvin got up and was getting ready to leave. "We could've had this conversation over the phone."

"Bruh, sit down and chill." Wes demanded. "That's probably part of your problem—you're so uptight that you are letting that little divorce you're going through interfere with your ability to relate to the students."

"I'm not uptight," Calvin sat back down. He was going to give Wes a chance to clean up the situation.

"Then watch me bust this white chick real quick," Wes snapped his fingers quickly two times.

Calvin watched as the blonde Kim Kardashian look-alike waltz over and gave Wes a big hug. Her friend—the one that looked like Paris Hilton tried to find her spot next to Calvin.

"What's your name?" The woman asked him.

Before he could open his mouth to speak, he could tell that her eyes were focused a couple of feet below his face. He knew she was trying to size him up in the slacks he was wearing.

Calvin wished he had on some baggy jeans and a back pack.

"My mama named me Calvin—and my wife calls me her man," Calvin got smart in a tone that let her know that he wasn't interested.

"My mama named me Christine," she licked her fuchsia-colored lips. "But peoples call me Cream."

It didn't take Calvin long to figure out what was really going one. "That's what's up. What's with the blonde wig? I bet you look better in brown or black."

"I agree. But I'm on a clock and Madame Mulah don't play," Cream confirmed. "That's how these golden tresses made it to the crown on my head. Not much I can do about that—I know my place."

"Where's your client?" Calvin looked around to see if anyone was searching for someone.

"Supposed to be you," Cream pointed at him.

Calvin looked around and saw Wes intimately entertaining the woman in his seat. Calvin shook his head and could hide the frustration on his face.

"I hate to break it to you but this ain't that kind of party and I'm not that kind of man."

"Don't worry," Cream was confident when she tried to move in on Calvin. She lowered her hand to reach into Calvin's pants but he blocked her. She rolled her eyes and smacked her lips in disappointment, "your date has already been paid for. I'm with you the rest of the night."

"Oh word?" Calvin gave Wes the side eye as he saw his boy's face nuzzled in the lady's neck.

"Word. I see this chump you with didn't inform you what the deal was. I'd thought you be game. I like for all of my clients to have a good time."

"We can still have one. Follow me," Calvin got up and instructed Cream to do the same.

Calvin just knew that he and Wes were going to have a conversation. He also knew that the bar was not the time nor place. He wondered why Wes would disrespect him like this but decided that he'd use the opportunity to do something positive.

"Are we going to your room?" Cream was anxious to get the party started.

"What room?" Calvin shook his head. Out of the corner of his eye, he saw Wes take his date by the hand and lead her away and he knew that Cream would want to follow suit. "Hold on a minute—Wes, let me holla at you for a minute."

Calvin looked on as Wes took his date's hand and kissed it. As the two of them stepped to the side, he saw where Wes' girl couldn't take her eyes off of him. Under different circumstances, Calvin would've left Wes right where he was posted.

"Wes—you bought a hooker?"

"No, I just dropped a couple of dollars on a lady who can show you a good time."

"Wes—this ain't my type of party," Calvin was clearly frustrated. Controlling his anger was becoming more and more of challenge as the seconds went on. Wes didn't know it but "bruh" was in danger. "And you know what kind of man I am."

"I do," Wes said barely above a whisper. "But I assure you Jesus wouldn't mind if you released some tension every once in a while. Have you looked at yourself in the mirror lately—you look backed up."

"How I look—never mind." Appalled, Calvin didn't want the answer to that question. "What room is this Cream chick talking about?"

"Look, I got us adjoining rooms at this hotel on Sugar Creek Parkway. When you get tired of her or I get tired of Cinnamon, we'll switch."

Calvin was speechless. The words he wanted to say couldn't bring themselves to release from his lips.

"Man loosen up," Wes put his arm around his shoulder. With his other hand, he put a key card in Calvin's hand. "Go to the room—wear her out. Bang the walls, sing praises—whatever you got to do so you can do your thing because I really want you to keep your job. I'd hate to lose another black teacher because there aren't enough of us as it is."

Calvin couldn't believe his ears. Wes was crazy if he thought he was going to have sex with the prostitute. Calvin looked at the monitor that was above the bartender and he couldn't believe what he saw the news brief. "Ayo, turn that up please?" Calvin commanded as he slyly slid a twenty dollar bill to the lady working the bar. The lady smiled at him and did what was requested. Calvin watched Stuart Scott and some of the other announcers talk about one of the upcoming college games.

"Let's do the thing champ."

Calvin reluctantly followed Wes back to the bar and soon, followed his boss to the parking lot so he could follow him to the hotel. He looked around to make sure no one recognized the two of them then he unlocked the door to his car to allow Cream inside.

***

It was obvious what was going on in the next room but for Calvin, he was caught up in a bigger battle of his own.

"Jesus did not speak with prostitutes," Cream rebuked with excitement.

"Jesus' disciples came from all walks of life—a tax collector, fishermen. And Jesus preached to the sinner and those 'regular church folk' if you could call them that."

Calvin decided that since the room was paid for and the woman would be in his company for awhile, he'd use the opportunity to save a soul. Or return a backsliding Christian to her first love. Whatever the case may be—he was going to use the hotel room for good.

Cream gave him an entry way when she picked up one of the devotions that was lying in the passenger's seat in the car. Calvin had left them there after going door to door to minister to souls with the other Street Disciples. He'd meant to take the copies to Bible Study last night but the tests he was grading took longer than anticipated.

Calvin read the story about Mary Magdalene and pointed out in his study Bible that and the other references to prostitutes whom found salvation through Jesus.

"But if I give this up, where is my money going to come from?"

"You just sat here and told me that you got a degree in Accounting—why aren't you using it?"

"I am—I handle Madame Mulah's financial operations. I'm paying off a debt right now."

"Well—Jesus paid a debt in blood that cost more than you owe to whomever you are in debt to."

Calvin watched as Cream thought for a minute. Cream got up and took the sheets off the bed and then she placed herself in the middle of it and read the devotional. Calvin reached into his black sports bag and pulled out a small pocket Bible that he traveled with from time to time. "Read the Bible passage that goes along with the devotional."

Cream took the Bible from Calvin's hand and she opened it. After glancing at it for a few minutes, she passed it back. "What's with the the's, thou's, shalt's and these other words we don't use no more. How am I going to follow something I don't understand?"

"God's word is timeless. There's a New Revised Standard Version, an International Version, a New King James Version. A bunch of translations that people read that have modern words. I just don't have one. But if you let me, I'll go to the car and get you one. It's been written in and highlighted but the material is good."

"I'll be waiting on you."

Calvin grabbed the room key and rushed to the car. He hadn't wanted to—but he felt at peace with the idea of giving Cream his personal Bible. He knew that he could get another copy and that by time he read most of the passages again—he'd get something different than what he had read before.

When he got back to the room, he saw Wes exiting with just a towel wrapped around his waist.

"You a silent lover?" Wes asked him.

Calvin scrunched his face. He couldn't understand why Wes would have a preoccupation about how he handled his business.

"I'm putting in work," Calvin told a half-lie. Calvin was working on Cream's salvation—leaving out the part that the work didn't involve him taking off his clothes and breaking a sweat.

"Cinnamon is wearing me out," Wes bragged. "You want to switch or you good? I kind of want to get a taste of Cream."

"I'm good," Calvin headed to his room, "I'm not done with her yet."

"Well, when you get done just knock on the door."

Wes walked into his room and Calvin into his. He was thankful that Cream was still dressed and that she was still into the devotional by time he returned. Calvin knew he would be able to resist the temptation for the rest of their time together and possibly win over a new convert to Christ.

Chapter Twenty-Four

Friday, October 31, 2008
Calvin's Bedroom
Winston-Salem, North Carolina
5:11 PM

"Man!" Calvin moaned as he struggled to collect himself as he slowly hopped up out of the bed. Deitrick Haddon was encouraging him to count his blessings even with the migraine stomping his head.

His breaths were worse than the chronic asthma attacks he suffered as a child. He brought his hand to his chest slowly to pace the beat of his heart—it was rapidly going faster, rivaling the beat of the 808s used in a classic So So Def production.

Every time he had the same vision—nightmare—he could feel in his spirit that something wasn't right. But to have the vision today was odd.

In a few hours, he'd be getting on a plane to bring his brother home. He wondered if what he was feeling was guilt. Calvin knew his brother had forgiven him as he forgave his brother but still—fourteen years was a long time for an innocent man to pay for the crime of another—even if it was his brother.

Calvin closed his eyes and had the same vision all over again.

"Raise up fool!" Garfield issued the challenge to Carlton when he and his boys, Freddie, Tony and Cedric reached the park.

Carlton had been talking to a young lady he had met at the Albertsons grocery store a block away—plotting on how the two of them were going to get into some mischief later on that day. Calvin hadn't been too far—had just come out of the house after eating a snack and was looking to get Carlton and a few of the neighborhood kids together so they could walk to the next apartment complex over and challenge them to a basketball game.

"If I had known you lived here I would have come by to finish off you and your brother." Garfield threatened.

Calvin though about their last violent encounter—they were at the playground of the elementary school his younger brother Casey had went to. Garfield had accused Carlton of messing around with his girl. The allegations were true but Carlton never admitted to it. Calvin was old enough to understand the kind of woman that Garfield was messing with but didn't have the heart to call her a Jezebel.

A fight that started out between Garfield and Carlton soon became unfair as Freddie and Cedric jumped in. Calvin, being of height and weight disadvantaged, threw his sticks and stones in the affray with the big boys and just as Carlton was getting tumbled, Calvin found himself getting beat too.

A gun brandish by another one of their friends, Tony had kept them back and when it was all said and done, the gun ended up in Garfield's hands and when it went off, Sammie, the younger brother of Calvin's friend, Lester, ended up with a bullet in his head at the school he attended kindergarten.

By time Calvin was brought back to the present, he caught Carlton had delivered two quick blows to Garfield's dome. Garfield ducked back and Carlton followed with two more punches and quickly tripped him.

Calvin got excited when Garfield fell on his back and Carlton capitalized on his advantage, throwing more blows to his face.

"Get that mofo!" Calvin yelled in excitement. The taste of revenge was sweet and he was vowing to jump in if any of Garfield's friends kept the fight from being fair.

Carlton was going to work like Mike Tyson on an unworthy contender until Garfield lifted his foot up and kicked him in the groin. Carlton crouched down and Calvin rushed to Garfield and threw two face blows before the big bully could get up. Garfield wasted no time scooping Calvin up like a rag dog.

Being over Garfield's shoulder was not where Calvin wanted to be, but seeing the chrome Glock that was in the back of Allen's pants made the trip worth it. As Allen and Cedric brought their fight closer to Calvin—he thinking quickly snatched it up and gripped it tightly before Garfield tossed him on the ground.

Carlton attacked Garfield from behind and soon, the two were on the ground wrestling. After the shock of being slammed to the ground wore off, Calvin jumped up and ran to the fight. He lifted the gun up and smacked Garfield in the face.

Watching Garfield reach for his face and fall to the ground wasn't enough. Calvin looked at the gun again and associated the weapon with power. He pulled the trigger and the force from the gun almost caused him to drop it.

A sinister grin came on Calvin's face. He walked toward Garfield, basking in glory in watching the older bully cower and try to back away.

"Calvin, tell me that's not my piece?" Calvin heard Allen yell an explicative.

Calvin snickered wickedly as he watched Allen feel around for the piece he was holding for an older Blood member. "Don't worry, you'll get it back. I'm just gonna do this real quick."

"I don't have no bodies on that one man," Allen lied, "you need to give that back."

"Shut up!" Calvin was done negotiating as he struck Garfield again.

"Calvin, give me the gun," Carlton tried to reason with Calvin, "I done already whooped his butt twice already. He ain't gonna mess with us no more."

"Naw," Calvin shook his head and steadily aim the gun at Garfield's face again, "I'm a kill this fool just like he killed Carla. And then I'm get at his boys."

"Don't kill this fool in broad daylight man," Allen tried to reason with him, "Look at all these witnesses you got out here. You'll go to prison with the grown folks and you'll never get out."

Calvin wasn't trying to hear that. In his mind, a couple of years in juvie was worth the price of getting revenge on the man that not only killed his older sister, but the little boy who broke all of their hearts.

"I don't care if I go to prison. I care about avenging my sister's death. Only thing I hate is that Cola's ain't out here so I can finish her off too."

"Yo, Cal, just because Garfield is a Crip doesn't mean that he killed Carla." Carlton tried to reason with Calvin but it was no use. Calvin was off the deep end.

"He did!" Calvin yelled as he glared at Garfield. The way he and his nemesis locked eyes confirmed the truth between the two of them. "I always knew this sucka was behind Carla's death. Ever since she's been gone I could feel it every time I see this cat. I don't feel it around Tony or Cedric or them other Crips. I feel it with him and I don't like it. But as soon as I pull this trigger, I won't feel it no more. And don't think I haven't forgotten about Sammie either!"

Garfield looked down. We all knew about Sammie because with the exception of Second, Allen and his crew, we all were there when that happened. Garfield sat Indian style and just looked at Calvin.

"Cola was never Carla's friend. I was just using that dumb broad to get at Carla so I could get at her man. Don't act like you didn't know who Carla's man was and don't act like she wasn't a Blood because she was," Garfield tried to defend himself but Calvin wasn't trying to hear that. In his mind, all he needed to know was that Garfield killed Carla.

"Carla wasn't no Blood," Allen said. "Carla didn't even like us like that. She loved De'Angelo for the man he was and he loved her for the woman she was. They fought all the time because he wanted her to be down with the set, but she just wasn't down like that. The only person you ever seen Carla roll with like that was Cola and that was because she really looked at Cola like a sister. We tried to tell her about Cola and Cola being a Crip and all of that, but she wasn't trying to hear us. Between being worried about if she was going to Spellman and being with her man, she couldn't see Cola for what she really was, a trifling, snake trick! Carla had hopes of getting out of here and marrying her man because she really thought she could get him out of the *game and change him. If Carla was wrong for anything, she was wrong for believing that."*

"Whatever man, you just covering for her. But you know what, I killed that trick because she was with the wrong man, at the wrong place and at the wrong time and as soon as I get up, I'm going to kill this punk and his brother too!"

"Reach for yours then!" Calvin challenged.

For a minute, he thought he was in a Western. He watched as Garfield backed away and stood up and quickly drew for his. Garfield pulled it out and without warning, the two men shot at each other. Garfield was falling down and Calvin shot another shot at his heart. This time, the bullet was faster and just ripped through Garfield chest and came out coated with crimson blood. Calvin aimed at Garfield's face and just before he landed on the ground, a bullet landed in his head.

"I told you I was quick." Calvin gloated as he threw the gun down on the ground next to Garfield. He turned his head in Allen's direction, "you can have your gun back."

Allen waved his hand and acted like he was pushing it away, "It's yours now. I don't want it."

Carlton walked up and just as we could hear the police sirens, he picked up the gun and shot another shot at Garfield's body. Carlton rubbed his bare hand on the gun and held the gun down towards his side.

"What are you doing?" Allen yelled.

"If anyone asked, I did this," Carlton said, crying. Calvin's eyes got big when he realized what his brother was doing. He started to reach for the gun, but someone was holding him back. "You guys hear me, I did this!"

The police came through the crowd and they ordered Carlton to put the gun down and to lie on the ground. Carlton did as he was told and the police rushed in, handcuffed him and picked him.

Tears fell from Calvin's eye as he heard the police make crude remarks. They cuffed and arrested Carlton and as they were escorting him away, Carlton looked at Martin, "watch after my brother man. Make sure he stays out of trouble. Do that for me and I'll owe you."

The police laid a white sheet over Garfield's body and marked the grass. Another set of plain clothes police officers took pictures and picked up gun shells and collected evidence. Casey was crying and Calvin took him and Martin's younger brother from the girls. Calvin sat on the curve and was crying. Calvin looked up and Carlton grinned at him.

"Stay out of trouble man, I got this. That's all you got to do."

Calvin watched as the police put Carlton in the back of their car and drove off. He reached for Casey and held him tight. Calvin shot his way into a new responsibility, that of being the bigger brother.

Calvin blindly followed Martin to his apartment. His bloodied shirt told the tale of a battle he was too young to be in. In the back of his mind, he was happy that he'd killed Garfield but he wasn't ready for the price his brother was getting ready to pay.

The phone rang for the umpteenth time and Calvin knocked over everything to get to the Palm. MARTIN LITTLE blared across in capital letters and he knew that his best friend was just calling to check on him.

He knew he wouldn't have to worry about the man walking in on him. Calvin pressed the TALK button. "Sup," he spoke with clarity.

"You're still having those dreams aren't you?"

Calvin hated the fact that Martin knew him so well. "I just pray that once we get Carlton home, that the nightmares would end."

"They'll end. Start rebuking them dreams in the name of Jesus."

"I did," Calvin sounded defeated. He prayed a thousand times over—but the murder would always seem fresh on his mind.

Martin had said some other stuff but Calvin struggled to keep up with him as Martin seemed to have spoken a thousand words a minute—his words were foreign like Spanish, a language Calvin barely understood. He checked the television to make sure he didn't roll over the remote and put it on Telemundo by mistake.

"You get Carlton's last letter," Calvin had finally understood Martin. "He said he sent you one and you didn't respond."

"No," Calvin responded dryly. Calvin was under so much pressure between not doing well in graduate school and the drama with his school that he didn't remember Carlton's letter. "Nothing's wrong is there?"

Calvin silently recited the prayer. *"Our Father who art in heaven —hollowed be they name—thy kingdom come—thy will be done—on earth as it is in heaven—"*

"You need to be walking out of the house in an hour. I'm serious. I'm not trying to be late for our flight," Martin yelled out. Apparently Calvin had missed some of Martin's conversation.

Calvin walked to his dresser to grab some fresh underclothes and went to the bathroom to take a shower and prepare to get on the late evening flight. He glanced at the mirror, one last time before he made a dash to the bathroom. Calvin washed his body in record time and put on the under clothes—thankful that he had set out what he was going to wear at the airport after praying with Cream and helping her seek salvation the night before. Wes wasn't too happy about that but he didn't have long to contemplate because after having a few hours for the teacher workday, he was free to make sure his brother was home for good for the weekend.

Calvin opened the bottle of mouthwash and took a few sips. He did a quick swish, spit and expelled the wash from his mouth. He put on the clothes that were hanging on the back of the bathroom door. As he ran out of the bedroom, he stopped for a brief moment to pick up a travel bag that he had prepared for Carlton. In a few days, his brother would be living with him. He looked into the spare bedroom and despite the mild depression, he and Martin were able to make sure that the room looked presentable. Calvin quickly retrieved his keys and raced out of the apartment.

Calvin's Bedroom

Winston-Salem, North Carolina

6:11 PM

Martin was smiling when he seen Calvin adjusting his shirt when he stepped out of the car.

"Man, I didn't think you was gonna make it," Martin gave Calvin a pound. Calvin also gave a friendly grip to Franklin and Mike. Franklin had grown up with Calvin and Martin in Denver and was the first to move to Winston-Salem. It was here where he met Mike, a straight-acting homosexual who had no problems letting him or anyone else know that he was more man than any Olympian or muscle bound dude could have ever hoped to be. At first, Calvin wasn't feeling the idea of Franklin being cool with Mike like that but once he saw that Mike wasn't going to "make Franklin gay," or turn him out as they say now, Calvin stopped tripping. Of course, the fact that Mike stood up to him during his freshman year at college for accusing him of being "soft" followed by a very stern and disciplining letter from Carlton helped out too.

"I've been waiting over thirteen years for my brother to get out of that joint," Calvin pressed the lock button on his keypad and walked with his friends to Martin's black 2007 Nissan Altima. It was hard to believe that Martin had had the car for over a year and it still had that fresh new car smell. "I can't wait to bring him home.

The young men started their journey by traveling twenty five miles east on I-40. They listened to Michael Baisden try to talk some sense into some caller who felt that black people were not intelligent enough to be entrepreneurs. That conversation hit a cord with both Martin and Mike as they both were successful business owners in their own right. Martin was a writer who owned his own publishing house that specialized in publishing Christian Fiction for both adults and teens. He was also a partner in a small barbershop. Mike served as executive director of a group home for troubled gay teens and owned a small club and entertainment center that hosted gospel concerts and talent shows which he allowed high school and college students to intern so they could get a taste of the entertainment industry.

"How she gonna say black people can't run a business?" Mike complained. "Yeah, we're not all drug dealers with our pants off our behinds wearing Timbs and jewelry off our necks."

"Yeah, a lot of times folks assume that if we're black business people that we're either selling drugs or bootlegging videos," Martin added.

"Or that we're dishonest businessmen trying to rip folks off."

"You know what the problem is though?" Martin proposed, "When there is a shady brother or sister out there not honoring their contracts or playing games with peoples' money because they got emotional issues, they make it bad on all of us."

"We need to start holding our brothers and sisters who do bad business accountable instead of blowing off all the other brothers and sisters in the business and not giving them a chance to do the right thing." Mike added.

The men continued to listen as Michael Baisden and his guest educated others about the importance of reinvesting and supporting African American owned businesses. Once they arrived at the airport, they checked in, relaxed a little and boarded their plane.

***

"So what happened with you and Kima?" Calvin knew it would be a matter of time before Martin tried to get the 411.

Calvin declined the hard liquor offered in favor of the can of ginger ale from the flight attendant who winked at him. He looked at the Nicki Minaj-shaped beauty and knew that in a few minutes, he was going to renig on his celibacy vow. The way she moved slowly and seductively had him tempted. Calvin knew he was going to decline her offer to join her for a mile high ritual.

"I was a respectable Christian man," Calvin responded sharply while glancing at Martin out of the side of his eye. "How were you and Keisha?"

Calvin took a sip of ginger ale and couldn't help but chuckle at witnessing Martin looking at the flight attendant and comparing her shape to the bottle in his hand. Martin licked his full lips the way LL did in his videos and they both caught her giggling at him as she talked to another flight attendant. The other flight attendant was giving Maliah Michele, the stripper Drake was always rapping about a run for her money.

"Keisha might be the one..." Martin replied, struggling to peel his eyes away from the two beauties. "I'm gonna try her out for a few more months and see where it goes. I already introduced her to mom and pops and plus she knows a little something about hair herself even though she's going to be a makeup artist."

"But I bet what's on your mind right now is figuring out how you can have the both of them," Calvin enjoyed another sip of his drink. He'd never admit to Martin the thought flashed in the back of his mind.

"Naw, it's not even like that that," Martin finally peeled away. "I'm focused on Keisha. She sells beauty products for M. Walker like my dad and she works with some local news anchors making sure they look right before they step into the limelight."

Calvin cut right to the chase, "you feeding me some bull man."

"Why you say that?"

"You not sleeping with her?"

Martin got dead silent because he knew the answer to that question was that they have had intercourse a time or two but they also agreed to remain celibate until they walked down that aisle, and made a promise to God to honor each other as man and wife. Martin also knew it was his fault for the line of questioning. So he answered the question the best way he knew how without bringing dishonor to Keisha, "we decided to wait until Holy Spirit brings us into that unity with Jesus."

"I'm not gonna front, Kima and I almost did it," Calvin made sure that Martin was looking him in the eye. "We really took it there, butt naked and everything. Just when I was about to put it in, all I could see was my wife and how wrong *I* would be if *I* did that to *her.*"

"Don't beat yourself up over it man," Martin could tell it was eating at Calvin that he almost gave into his flesh and fed it what it desired. "Rev. McClurkin was right, we fall down but we get back up again."

"I mean, I was *this* close to physically committing adultery," Calvin emphasized by bringing his index finger and his thumb about face and making sure there was very little space inbetween.

"I'm not one to talk about committing adultery—you done already seen me do that." Calvin briefly flashed back to a time where Martin was dared to have sex with an ex-girlfriend of his, and also remembered the scolding that Martin had received from his father because he hadn't abstained from sex. "Sometimes, I find that as Christians, we're not able to move forward because we keep reminding God about what we did. God will forgives us for it and then when we bring it right back to him he's like 'huh.'"

"You right," Calvin and Martin stopped talking long enough to take the drink and the peanuts from the stewardess. "You think God's gonna forgive that Maria and I got a divorce."

"I can't answer that one." Martin took a sip and then continued, "but I feel that if you know that you made the best effort to save your marriage, you will be okay. I mean, you stayed with her after you discovered that she was messing around on you with another man, you tried to spend time with her, you tried to go to counseling with her. She left you in the middle of the night and Lord knows what she could have drugged you with."

"You think I was drugged?"

"You said yourself that you've never been a heavy sleeper ever since Garfield…" Martin stopped because he knew that he reminded Calvin of the afternoon when he took that young man's life. True, Garfield, being the leader of the Crips at his middle school was a true terror, but still, his life was gone and he did not have the opportunity to turn his life around or to get help. After a few years and with some counseling, Calvin learned to forgive himself for that and for the fact that he was responsible for putting his brother in jail. "You never sleep light. You used to wake me up paranoid when we stayed in the dorm."

"But I'm getting better with that though."

"Yeah?"

"Yeah."

Martin and Calvin continued to talk until their plane landed at Denver International Airport. The airport looked like it fit in with the Rocky Mountain backdrop. They later rejoined Franklin and Mike as they got their stuff and their rental car and left the airport.

Saturday, November1, 2008
Darren's Mini-Mansion
Denver, Colorado
11:45 AM

176 broken but i'm healed

The four young men enjoyed their stay at a nice five bedroom house in the Hidden Valley area that was owned by the award winning actor Darren Colbert. Darren was a tall, six foot nine dark chocolate A-list actor who had also sold candy with the boys when they were kids. He had already sent Martin the keys to his house and would be flying in this morning before they were to leave to pick up Carlton from jail. Darren had just finished shooting a scene for an upcoming movie based off one of a novels Martin had written when he was in college.

This morning, they were greeted by their mixed race, black and Mexican friend Juan Morales. Back in the day, he was the shortest one in the crew and was picked on for speaking both Spanish and English to his friends. Now, he is the second tallest at six foot five. After spending a stint in a homeless shelter, he focused on redeveloping his basketball skills, eventually being able to play college and professional basketball overseas. His three children who were all elementary school-aged were well mannered and his wife was working in the kitchen, making sure, "her men" as she liked to refer to them were well fed.

The only ones in the middle school crew that were missing were the twins Ray & Trey. No one really knew what had happened to them. Word on the street was that they were caught up in the gang violence and possibly ended up behind bars. No one had been successful at locating them and finding out where they really were.

Last year, Martin, Calvin, Franklin, Mike and his partner, Eric, had went to Colorado to bury their other friend Lester next to his little brother Sammie. They had made an attempt to get special permission for Carlton to be released temporary since Lester and Calvin's families were close, but the State of Colorado wasn't budging. That was a rough time for all of them because they knew that Lester's desire to defend our country from terrorism grew more so out of his perceived lack of ability to protect Sammie from getting killed by Garfield on an elementary school playground. That event was the catalyst for the war they waged against the gang when they were sixth graders and what eventually led to Calvin and Garfield having their shootout. Carlton had requested that they visit Lester and Sammie's gravesite before going to meet with family and friends so that he could pay them their respects.

Their other friends that they were able to keep up with in Winston-Salem, Second and Brenda, were enjoying married life with their children and had agreed to stay back to help prepare the home that Carlton would be moving into.

As they finished eating and reminiscing on their youth in Colorado, they made the two hour trip to the correctional facility that Carlton was being released from. Everyone was giddy with joy until they arrived at the big gray building that was protected by barbed wire and steel. Calvin thought about Abednego and his ministry working with young men in prison and remembered the parable that the good seeds were to grow with the bad and they should be separated at the Harvest. Calvin had often wondered how many lives were not given a chance to be cultivated behind bars because the rehabilitation that was supposed to take place wasn't to be. He thought about how common it was to see these young men on the corner, being misunderstood people who ministers, political leaders and others who claimed to profess Christianity or some "other faith" refused to give them the light. Only if Kanye could have given them the feeling.

The men were getting out of a white 2007 Yukon and they watched the peanut butter and caramel colored man leave the correctional facility for good. The folded brown bag held all of his worldly processions and in his right hand, the Word of God gave him the encouragement to put a little extra pep in his step. The taste of freedom that he hadn't had since he was a youth began to remind him of all the foods he wanted to partake in once he got home. Juan's wife had agreed to cook a down home southern meal and had enlisted the help of her sisters to make sure that they had a feast fit for a king.

Calvin met up with his parents at the gate and gave them a hug. They were enjoying their lives in Phoenix, Arizona and had tried to convenience Carlton to go back with them, but Carlton had a goal of pursuing divinity school at Shaw University. First, he wanted to attend Winston-Salem State University as his brother and Martin had.

One of the pictures that Rahliem had sent him fell out of the Bible and Carlton kneeled down cautiously to pick it up. It would be a while before the custom and culture of prison life would wear off of him. He had given Calvin and everyone else a first taste of what they would be dealing with upon their return to Winston-Salem. And that was another joy Carlton had about getting out of jail, joining Rahliem's Street Disciples Ministry and spreading the Word and the good news of Christ in the streets as he did in the prison once he got saved three years ago. Once he had gotten saved, he had worked on both Calvin and their little brother, Casey's salvation. Casey was the easier case because he was pursuing a professional bowling career, which had very little African Americans involvement and had very little support on a national level when compared to sports like tennis, golf and lacrosse. Casey himself didn't look bad bearing an ironic and striking resemblance to Tiger Woods, making his goal to be the Tiger Woods of bowling that much easier.

Carlton became living proof that God, when given the opportunity to try him, can change any situation you *think* you are in and make it out for your good. True, he spent over thirteen years in jail for a crime he didn't commit, but when he thought about the children he hadn't fathered when he was getting with any woman who would give it up and baby mama drama that normally comes along with such responsibilities, or the STD's he didn't catch from having numerous unprotected sex encounters at a young age, prison wasn't such a bad thing.

Carlton gave his mother a long hug once he finally reached her and their father, Calvin and Casey joined in. Calvin shed tears of joy because his brother was finally free.

Chapter Twenty-Five

Everyone was getting into their cars after paying respects to Lester and Sammie. Just as suspected, Sammie's murder brought back fresh memories of that eventful day, but they rejoiced and healed knowing that both Sammie and Lester were with Jesus.

"I can't wait to taste some good food," Carlton said in a rich, high voice reminiscent of the comedian Katt Williams.

"My wife got it for you," Juan bragged. "You know her and her sisters can throw down in the kitchen."

"I believe it because her mother could cook," Carlton was excited.

"Yeah, she'd try to get you fattened up too so you could stop being a Casanova."

"Oh that's what that was."

Everyone enjoyed a laugh in the Yukon. The men continued to go down memory lane and talk about their days of selling candy. The teased each other about the girls they liked and the women they were dating now. Once they got to Darren's house, Calvin pulled Carlton to the side so he could have a short one on one with his big brother.

"You know why Maria is not here?" Calvin was hoping that he would not have to have this discussion with Carlton upon his release, but he thought it better now to get it out of the way.

"I know," Carlton confirmed, pulling out a letter that Maria had handwritten and handed it to Calvin. "She told me about Bilal and her reasons for wanting a divorce from you."

"I can't believe that…"

"It's no reason to get mad Calvin. I look at it like this. I know you are worried about whether or not what you are doing is the Christian thing to do. I say, let go and let God."

"I try but…"

"I thought you learned that poem about excuses."

"I did."

"Look at it this way…she's using Bilal as an excuse to do whatever it is she is setting out to do with her life at this time. She may come to realize that she made a mistake. You on the other hand, have to wake up every day with the desire to be a better man for the Lord than you were yesterday. Being a Christian means that you are free from being a slave to sin…it does not mean that you won't go through trials and tribulations or that you are immune to them. You remember that song at the end of *Diary of a Mad Black Woman* that Pattie LaBelle sings about being free?"

"What you know about *Diary of a Mad Black Woman?*"

"Boy you silly," Carlton grabbed Calvin and put him in a headlock, "I also know that if I was a woman, Mo'Nique could've been my cellmate too. Anyway, I love Tyler Perry and what that man is about and I can't wait to buy the DVDs and go the movies and support the plays."

"You must have been in the car with us before we got on the plane to get here."

"Who do you think has been schooling Martin and Mike about business?"

Calvin looked at Carlton and shook his head. He glanced at his hand and realized it had been bare for a week now. It was the longest that he's ever gone without wearing his wedding ring ever since the pastor declared him and Maria husband and wife and he kissed his bride. Calvin began to realize what his brother was trying to do other than get inside the house so he could get him some southern food to eat. On one hand, without the ring, Calvin was free to pursue a stronger relationship with God and to grow more within himself in Christ. On the other hand, Calvin was free to love Maria in a new way—to love her as his sister in Christ and as the woman she was destined to be.

Chapter Twenty-Six

Wednesday, November 5, 2008
Tenth & Patterson Homeless Shelter
Winston-Salem, North Carolina
6:30 PM

Calvin and Cream finished their volunteer up their work and got ready to leave.

"So how did you like being out here?"

The Street Disciples Ministry group and a few of their friends had just got done serving the homeless men and women and afterwards partaken of the leftovers.

"I thought being a Christian meant going to church, quoting scripture and then beating everyone else in the head who doesn't love the Lord."

"Naw—being a Christian is so much more than that. We are to do the work as part of the Body of Christ. God works quite a few of his miracles through us."

Calvin started gathering his things. Cream had a relative here and wanted to see Calvin's group in action ever since he'd talked to her about salvation a few weeks ago. Cream had told him earlier that she was considering moving to the Tre-Four so that she could avoid some of the people who could take her back into prostitution.

"So you are coming to Bible Study on Thursday aren't you?"

"Yeah. I'm nervous though, I haven't been in church in a long time. I don't even know where my Bible is. I hope God isn't mad."

"God is not mad, I'm sure. We have Bibles at the church you can use. We can go to one of the Christian book stores and get one if you want."

"I would appreciate that a whole lot." Cream was excited but nervous. "Tell me something, Christians have a whole bunch of Bibles to use and I don't even know which one to get. Which one does this church use?"

"Well, it's not a matter of which one the church uses. The different versions are for the reader."

Calvin and Cream walk out of the center. Calvin said goodbye to some of the other members of the group and then walked to the trunk of his car. "Come here for a minute, I'll show you the difference."

"This whole becoming a Christian thing is nerve wrecking. I don't know what to do or where to go."

"Being a Christian is not easy. You're going to make mistakes, but that is when we lean on Jesus and ask for help in trying to get it right. Now I'm going to pull out three bibles but I don't have the fourth one. I know about three of them but I don't know much about the fourth so see, I got a lot to learn two."

"I thought you knew it all."

"Nope. Even I got to step back and learn from the teacher time from time. You see, there are many translations of the Bible. I am going to do my best to give accurate descriptions of each one so that you may know what is what and know where your pastor or television/radio minister is coming from."

"Okay. Who do you watch on television?"

"I try to catch Creflo Dollar when I can. Sometimes I pop in a Tyler Perry movie. Then there's Joel Osteen, but that is another lesson."

"Okay."

Calvin held up an old tattered Bible and handed it to Cream. "This is the King James Version. You're probably familiar with it. This is the oldest English version of the Bible and the one many of the versions are based on. This Bible was translated from the Hebrew, Greek and Latin texts in 1604 and published in 1611 under the authority of King James I of England. This version is the most heavily used in the churches because it is the most referenced."

Cream flipped through the pages, "my momma got one of these. I can't read or understand it. That old English got on my nerves. I couldn't believe that God talked like that.

"He doesn't," Calvin chuckled.

"Are you laughing at me?"

"I'm not laughing at you. I remember I used to think the same thing. I used to beg God and say 'speak English.' It wasn't until I visited my brother in prison that he told me what he learned about this Bible and I like to use it because I teach from it from time to time and I find that many people can understand what I'm saying."

Calvin hands her a paperback copy of the New Revised Standard Version of the Holy Bible. "This is the New Revised Standard Version. This version is based on different revisions of the American Standard Version, which is based on King James Version. This version puts the Bible in everyday English. I could give the book to a three year old and he would have no problems reading or understanding what he is reading. Many daily devotionals use this version of the Bible so that everyone can understand what is being said and written. A lot of American writers are starting to incorporate this version as well. I used to just read the King James Version and that alone. I had been so used to it and then would pretend I knew what I was reading. It wasn't until a pastor showed me where I was already reading and understanding the New Revised Standard Version until I decided to read it too. I have a better understanding with the New Revised Standard Version and it serves as a wonderful reference/ study guide."

"So that's why people bring two Bibles to church?"

"Yeah, there are people who find like to follow along with the pastor or whoever is speaking and they read the King James Version. A lot of people are accustomed to the King James Version because that is all they know. A lot of Bible Study book and devotionals quote from the New Revised Standard Version so that people don't feel the need to get a dictionary to read the Bible. There's nothing wrong with any of the versions. And it's okay if you just get one. Get what you feel comfortable with."

"What are the other Bibles?"

"Well, there is the International Version, which is a common English Language version for those who don't speak 'Americanized' English. This version is based on the King James Version as most English language Bibles are. And then there is the Amplified Version...I'm not going to lie, I don't know much about this version other than to say that Creflo Dollar uses this version in addition to The King James Version in his sermons. Let me come back with more research on this one."

"Y'all are not playing. You got to be armed and ready."

"You have to be because that's how Satan works. He knows all these Bibles better than most of us. *We got to know* so that when he adds a word here, takes out two words there—we don't fall for his trap. That's how he gets us, but that's another subject."

Calvin reached in his bag and pulled out a copy of *The Upper Room* and another daily devotional.

"You can have these. These are daily devotionals, which helps us read the Bible day by day. There are a lot of people who just read these getting started so they can get accustomed to reading the Bible. There is nothing wrong with that because being a

Christian is not a religion, it is a lifestyle. And he doesn't expect us to be perfect in that. God knows that some people are not going to read the Bible everyday. He also knows there are people who can't read their Bible's every day for whatever reason. That's why we have these aids to help us on the way. I always tell people to use these to get you started. You will find many different devotionals, as everyone and their momma has their own devotional."

Calvin and Cream share a laugh.

"If I were to promote just one, it would be *The Upper Room*. They got a website, www.upperroom.org. There are small compact versions as well as a large magazine version. They are printed bi-monthly and are written using everyday language and examples. I find that I can relate to the different situations."

"Wow, I feel like I'm back in school."

"With the Lord, you are always in school. That's part of the reason why we have the Holy Spirit to help us along the way."

"Who is he again?"

"Who's who?"

"The Holy Spirit. I know a little bit about God and Jesus, but I don't know nothing about this Holy Spirit."

"That's okay, let me give you this Bible." Calvin reached back and handed her a New Standard Revised Version. "Let me find it," he mumbles as he thumbed through to Acts. "There's so much in here and many place you can start, so I'll say this. Read the book of Matthew first, then read Acts. You can read Luke, Mark or John. But read Matthew for a little background information on Jesus and his miracles and parables. Then read Acts which goes in dept about the Coming of the Holy Spirit. I wish I could go more in detail but this is just to get you started. And if you need help, here is my number 489.4608, I'll be here."

"That's Alicia Keys number."

"Yep. She don't know it but she's helped me save a lot of folks with her plug. I see your bus."

"Thank you so much. I'm nervous."

"You'll be okay."

Calvin watched as Cream got on the bus. Cream sat in an empty seat on the bus. She opened the book and began reading Acts chapter two.

Chapter Twenty-Seven

Sunday, November 9, 2008
Prayerful Baptist Church
Lexington, North Carolina

Calvin took a seat next to Miguel's family. He was supposed to be paying attention to the lady reading the concerns of the church but he was still thinking about the school and his situation. A forced cough caused him to turn around and face the audience.

"If there are any visitors, we would like to welcome you to Prayerful Baptist Church." The lady reading the announcements said.

Calvin stood up and looked around the small congregation—maybe thirty people were in attendance at the most. Another small family walked in.

"We are welcoming visitors. Let us know who you are and what church you belong to and if you are a guest of anyone."

"I'm Calvin Rice…I live in Winston-Salem and attend Grace United Methodist Church where my pastor is Reverend Lauren Phelps. And I'm a guest of Miguel."

The church sang a welcome song and then one of the deacons moved service along—encouraging the congregation to give their tithes and offerings. The choir was singing "I Need You To Survive." Calvin smiled and sang along with the choir as he knew the words to the song. After the choir finished their song, they praised God for the tithes and offerings.

An older lady with salt and pepper hair and cinnamon-colored skin walked to the podium. Her robe flowed as if the wind were blowing behind her. "Today's reading will come from Matthew 7:1-5. When you have it stand and say amen."

Within a minute's time, most of the church has found the passage in the Bible and have stood for the reading of God's word.

"The King James Version says JUDGE not, that ye be not judge. For with what judgment ye judge, ye shall be judged: and with what measure ye mete, it shall be measured to you again. And why beholdest thou the mote that is in thy brother's eye, but considerest not the beam that is in thine own eye? Or how wilt thou say to thy brother, Let me pull out the mote out of thine eye; and, behold, a beam is in thine own eye? Thou hypocrite, first cast out the beam out of thine own eye; and then shalt thou see clearly to cast out the mote out of thy brother's eye.

"I feel led to talk about our love for one another and how we don't show that when we pass judgment on our fellow man. In reading that passage, I understand that I don't have the authority to pass judgment on anyone regardless of what they do. I may not agree with their actions, but I of all people have no right to judge anyone's actions. Church wouldn't you agree?"

Various members of the church "amen'd" and the pastor continued.

"I'm going to talk about myself for a minute. When I was a little girl in Denver, Colorado, I used to ride into downtown with my parents. We would see all of the homeless people sitting on the streets in the summer time. Some would ask for money. Others would be trying to pick up trash that the drivers would throw on the streets. Others would simply ask for food. My parents used to think that only bad people ended up homeless. So I began to see the homeless people that sat on the corners as bad people. I used to also see some of the prostitutes that would walk the streets sit down and hang out with the homeless people from time to time. I was old enough to understand that prostitution was wrong and when I saw them hanging out with the homeless, I assumed that the homeless had done something to put them out of their home. I used to watch other children stare at them as if they never understood why they were homeless. As I got older, I carried those thoughts with me, even when I went to seminary.

"It never once occurred to me that the homeless didn't choose to be homeless. That some of the women who had become prostitutes may have had families they were trying to take care of. I just assumed that once a bad person, always a bad person. In fact, I could see everyone else's situation just as clear, but I couldn't turn a mirror to my own situation. I was just like the homeless. Hanging out with my girls going from one party to the next party the next party. That led me from going to one house to the next house to the next house. And I became that prostitute, going from one man to the next man, to your man."

"Alright girl!" A woman stood in the crowd.

"But every day I got off the bus to go to my job, I thought because I was able to ride the bus to and from work; that I was at somebody's house waking up to some breakfast and getting out of someone's bed. I spent check after check after check buying Mac and Donna Karen and Elizabeth Taylor thinking that I was better than they."

"Well! Preach Pastor!" The church encouraged.

"I did. I turned my nose up at them. And I thought I was better than they were. But when you take away the perm that the beautician I was messing with who happen to be married put in my hair. When I think about the credit card bills sent to a post office box instead of an apartment that was in my name. When I let men have their way with me for a Happy Meal or some lobster or a ring or some jewelry or for the opportunity to go to a concert, I couldn't see who I really was. I don't think ya'll hear me."

A woman in the church stood up and Miguel's wife clapped.

"I was just as quick to call these people homeless and hookers. But everyday I looked in the mirror to put on my foundation, my eye shadows and my lipsticks and mascara, I could not see that I myself was a homeless prostitute. Yet I thought I was better than they were because I was waking up from someone's bed or floor.

"Now if you look a little further in Matthew 22:36-40, Jesus says that thou shalt love the Lord thy God with all thy heart, and with all thy soul, and with all thy mind. This is the first and great commandment. And the second is like unto it, Thou shalt love thy neighbor as thyself. On these two commandments hang all the law and the prophets.

"Well, that would explain why I couldn't love them, I didn't love myself. I didn't love God. I loved talking about God and pretending that I was honoring God. I thought I had my own special connection to God and could make deals with him as I please. I loved God so much that I refused to give the homeless money or a meal. I loved God so much that I didn't want to be in the same area as the hookers. I didn't see them as my neighbors. I thought I was in one social class when I was really in the same. So you see, you can't love your neighbor if you are passing judgment on him or if you think you are better than him because his sin is not your sin. All sin is equal in His eyes. See, what we may think of as a small sin, ultimately can lead to what we may think of as a big sin. That's how it starts. For me, it started with my thought that I was better than somebody. Then as I began to do things of the person I thought I was better than, I tried to fix their situations without thinking about my own. Then I wanted to run to my Bible and start throwing that in someone's face because I thought I knew it so well. Now there is nothing wrong with pointing out the sin and using the Bible to show *why* it is a sin, but most people don't do that. We take a passage an run with it. We use the passages to pass judgment on a particular situation instead of looking at the whole picture. That's why folks call us hypocrites when we begin to talk to them because they realize that we are just the same as they are. Only difference is that we go to church on Sundays—praying and speaking tongues. But going to church on Sundays, praying and speaking in tongues is not going to get you into heaven. It's what's in your heart, that you keep and practice that takes you there. So look at your neighbor and say I Love You."

"I Love You," the church repeated.

"I will not pass judgment on you."

"I will not pass judgment on you."

"I will not gossip about you."

"I will not gossip about you."

"I will love you as I love myself as I love God."

"I will love you as I love myself as I love God."

"Is there someone out there in the crowd that wants to know Jesus? Maybe you've made a judgment about Him based on what you see others do instead of what the word of God says. Or perhaps, you got some issues going on in your life but you can't see clearly, would you come forward. Give your life to Jesus, and accept him as your Lord and Savior. It is not too late to accept him in your minds and your hearts today."

Calvin saw the man who came in with the family walking toward the front. The congregation clapped when the man embraced the pastor and welcomed the new member into the Body of Christ

Prayerful Baptist Church Parking lot
Lexington, North Carolina

"Calvin Rice."

Calvin turned around and was trying to remember where he'd seen the man who was calling his name from.

"Kah-Kah," the skinny young man who was next to him was mimicking and pointing at him, "Kah-Kah."

Calvin was confused as to why the two young men were calling his name. They looked so much alike. Both were five foot ten, though one wore a muscular frame and the slower-minded one was very slim. They shared proud African features through their brownie-colored skin and their almond-shaped eyes and full lips.

"You have to excuse my younger brother," the more athletic man spoke. "Jester," the man spoke as he addressed the slim young man. Calvin noticed how the man looked Jester in his eye and the slightly crooked smile the skinny one wore. "I want you to go to the car, play that *Afro-Latin Party* CD you like while I speak to the man and stay out of trouble."

Jester started laughing and repeated the word, "play."

"Your brother is Autistic," Calvin noted.

"Good guess," the man said as he took off his jacket to reveal a sleeveless, muscle bound T-shirt.

"Who are you and why are you here?" Calvin asked in a low voice. He didn't like the idea that he'd been followed and had no earthly idea as to what the man in front of him wanted.

"Some call me The Exterminator—I tend to make problems disappear. But I'll let you call me by my given name, King Dunlap."

Calvin pondered for a minute. He remembered Maria mentioning his name but he had no idea as to what context. "Come again, how do I know you?"

"Slow down killer," King stepped closer to Calvin, "I just need to talk to you for a minute."

Calvin looked around to see where Miguel was and found that he was talking with other parishioners of the church.

"Dude," Calvin gritted, "you don't know me well enough to be calling me no killer."

"Garfield Armstrong. Spring of 1994. Trust me, when I'm looking for someone, I do my research. But you are not whom I'm after—I need to talk to your wife."

"Dude," Calvin couldn't believe this man was telling him his business. On alert, he balled his fist. "You don't have nothing to say to my wife."

"After how she left our son and had me raise him by myself for nine months of his life, I got a lot to say to Maria."

Calvin unballed his fist. Then he remembered the only conversation he and Maria had about King.

"Where's the little boy at now?"

"He's been dead for almost seven years now—I don't want to talk about it. I just want to talk to her. Look, I'm not trying to start no mess—the man that raised me is a pastor too so I definitely wouldn't start nothing with you at a church—especially not one your friend belongs to."

"Maria left me a few weeks ago. She's probably in Winston-Salem with that dude."

"You really are saved—if that had been me, I'd been beat the pulp out of that punk deacon. Trust and believe, he got his coming."

Calvin didn't like the way conversation was headed.

"If you see her," King took out a business card and handed it to Calvin, "ask her to get in touch with me. She and I got unfinished business and I want to handle it while we are on this side of the Kingdom."

"I didn't know you were a believer," Calvin challenged.

"We come in all shapes and sizes. Who knows, maybe I'll have my own Saul to Paul story one day—but right now, I got a l'il rapist I need to catch up with. Jester!"

Calvin looked in the direction of King's car and found the young boy sitting in the driver's seat of the car and talking to one of the teenage parishioners of the church.

"I'll catch up with you later—we'll be in touch."

Calvin watched King chase after his car. As Jester pulled in closer, he could be heard laughing and repeating a word that sounded like "sex." Calvin shook his head.

"You know that guy?" Miguel questioned as he came from behind.

"Naw—never seen him before a day in my life. But he knows Maria."

"He's not another man is he?"

"Not exactly. He and Maria had a history before I came along."

Calvin watched as King put the car in park and then strongly chastised the young man for the mischief he was causing. King took his belt off, gave his brother a few straps to the tail and then manhandled the young man until he was in the backseat of the car.

"Well. You are welcome to come with us for lunch. We can hang out for a little while before you go home and grade papers."

"I'm fine, but thank you."

Calvin headed toward his car to return home. He wanted see what information he could find on King Dunlap and make sure he'd be prepared for any future unannounced visits.

Chapter Twenty-Eight

Wednesday, November 12, 2008
Mr. Rice's Classroom
Charlotte, North Carolina

"Mr. Rice." Charlie asked as she barged into class. She had barely had two steps in the classroom before she started in with her demands, "please tell me we are doing something other than Word today. I feel like my eyes are getting ready to fall off from looking at that blue square with the big W in the middle. I think I got carpal tunnel from all of this typing."

Calvin had been standing as he had been loading the Jeopardy game on his computer so that it would show up on the Smart Board for the students to play.

"We are doing something other than Word today—we are going to play Jeopardy to review all of the subjects in the Word processing unit in preparation for your test tomorrow."

"About time," Charlie announced as she took her seat. Calvin gave her a very stern look before Charlie declared she was "sorry" and took a seat.

"Must you come to class all the time acting a fool?" Emily asked. "Some of us want to learn."

"Yeah, some of us want to learn," Austin repeated as if he were a tape recorder.

"Alright," Calvin stepped in, "let's not get too excited. We got a lot to review today." Calvin looked up and noticed that all twenty-four seats in his class was filled to capacity. "I want each row to break off into teams and we will start in one minute."

Once the program for Jeopardy had completely loaded, Calvin opened the review with a video from CNN he had found that talked about Microsoft releasing Windows 7. The video had used some of the vocabulary words from the word back that Calvin had on the wall in their promotion about how they made some of the features in the operating system and the programs better.

Calvin noticed the interest the students had and knew that this would be the perfect lead in to the game.

Calvin asked for and got three nicknames for the groups of students. After writing their names into the program, Calvin started the game.

The questions asked varied on the different aspects of the word processing program. Some of the students had an idea about how it worked but they did not know the correct terminology. Calvin gave points when the correct vocabulary was used and deducted points when incorrect terminology was used.

The questions varied on topics like title pages, outlines, table of contents, job applications, resumes, agendas, minutes and itineraries. In addition, some of the questions focused on how to create these documents or how the documents were used.

As the game progressed, Calvin noticed that only a few students from each of the groups would participate. He kept going because he was offering the review and it was on the students to get the information.

"Man, this game sucks." Charlie replied. Her team had the lowest number of points, in part because she either kept joking or the rest of the team didn't know the answers.

Calvin shook his head, ignored Charlie and proceeded with the next question. The team answered right and Calvin continued with the rest of the game.

"I wish we weren't playing this stupid game anymore." Charlie protested.

"If you feel that way," Calvin replied, "You are free to take one of the detention passes and stay there for the rest of the game. Everyone else is trying to study for their unit exam, which is ten percent of your grade."

"I don't give a flip about ten percent. I'm going to pass this class anyway."

Calvin reached for the detention slips, filled out one, and told Charlie to come get the pass so that he could continue working with the rest of the students.

"I'm not going nowhere. Man, this class is wack and you suck as a teacher."

"Then leave."

"Why, so you can continue to act like a teacher that knows what he's doing?"

"No, so you can quit acting like an ass and stop disturbing my class." The moment the words left Calvin's lips, he knew he was going to hear about it one way or another. The students oohed and awed with amazement. "But you take this pass and go act like a fool with the detention teacher—everyone else in the class has a right to obtain an education and to review so that they may be successful."

Charlie looked surprised—but then she smirked as she got up, took the pass and slammed the door on her way out. Calvin continued reviewing the rest of the unit without further incident.

US52 (Outside of Lewisville)

As Calvin drove the long distance to his lonely home, he prayed to God silently to help him come to terms that this was probably the last semester he'd get to teach at Butler J. Parker High School.

The one hundred and thirty mile roundtrip drive between school and home was starting to take a toll on him—that along with the stress of his pending divorce, going through the action plan and his inability to bring up his grades from graduate school. Being on the road for two and a half to three hours a day on top of working for eight and half to ten hours a day leaves little time for sleep or to partake in personal hobbies.

Calvin missed being able to do events with Grace United Methodist Church and barely got to enjoy having his brother home from prison. He missed several service events that he was able to do before working.

Then, there was the issue of panic attacks—which occurred frequently over the last six weeks. Calvin was in denial about it at first, but when his brother found him on the floor a week after being home—Carlton pressed for Calvin to make changes. No more Wendy's, CookOut or Burger King on the way to and from work. Also, Calvin couldn't be on I-85 all the time. Calvin discovered some more scenic routes as he discovered he needed more time to de-stress from working with the teenagers after classes.

Calvin had decided that he would prefer to continue living in Winston-Salem and would consider moving to Greensboro. Concord was too small for him and as for Charlotte—he wasn't feeling too many of the people he'd met from there. But the distance between his home and school allowed him to leave work at work and to **come** home and enjoy family with minimal stresses from work. That was his motivation to arrive at Butler J. Parker as early as he could and often stay later than 2:45, which was the earliest he could leave for the day. Not to mention, A&T was closer to his home; even with most of his classes being distance learning for now, when he would have to go to class, it was better to drive thirty minutes home to Winston and not sixty to seventy miles to Charlotte.

The Montell Jordan ringtone let Calvin know that Wes was calling him from his cell phone. He almost didn't want to answer it because he decided that he couldn't hang out with Wes anymore. Wes' idea of fun did not fit in with the direction the Spirit was leading Calvin to go. Nevertheless, he answered the phone before the call went voicemail.

"Sup Wes," Calvin called out after he put the phone on speaker.

"You called Charlie an ass? Really Calvin?"

Oh gosh—he knew Wes was not going to let that go.

"No, I said she was acting like an ass." Calvin clarified when he saw a sign for gas advertising $2.87 a gallon. He remembered when he first started that gas prices were about $2.50 to $2.65 cents a gallon. Toward the end of Spring 2008, gas prices reached $3.60 - $3.75 a gallon and threatened to surpass $4.00 a gallon.

"Doesn't matter what you said, you shouldn't have said the word *ass* period. Do you want your job Calvin?"

"Of course I want it." Calvin was offended. "I wouldn't be coming in early and staying later if I didn't. Nor would I be helping out with the football games or trying to get the FBLA chapter reactivated."

"You know Dr. Hewett doesn't like you—"

"I don't care—as long as I'm able to teach the students and get them ready for the VoCATS exam—whether Dr. Hewett likes me or not."

Calvin could picture Wes shaking his head. "Okay Calvin. You know, I really want to keep you as a teacher, but you are making this very difficult. You are still on a lateral entry license. You can't teach students to read in the classroom—."

"If my students can't read, then why are we here? Reading should be a priority. If the students can't read, then it's not fair to expect me to meet the goals that are set by the school and the state for the student success rate. I can't believe I'm getting into trouble for teaching a student how to read."

"Calvin—if you have another incident, things will be taken to the next level."

The phone disconnecting caused Calvin's heart to beat excessively. His breathing sounded like wheezing and his vision became blurry. Calvin reached over to the dashboard to put on the hazard lights, and struggled to push the button in all the way. He heard honking as he struggled to pull the car over to the emergency lane. After about a minute, he was finally able to pull the car over. He rolled the window down all the way and loosened the tie and the button up.

"Are you okay?"

Calvin turned to the driver's side and he was greeted by an older white man who appeared to be in his mid-to-late fifties.

"Panic—attack," Calvin struggled to confirm.

A sense of peace and security blanketed him as he unlocked the door. The good Samaritan opened the door and immediately Calvin felt his breathing improved.

"Stressful day at work?" The man asked as he stood over Calvin.

Calvin shook his head yes.

"Where are you going?"

"Home—North Winston-Salem."

"Concord is a long ways from there to be teaching."

Calvin's eyes grew wide as he wondered how the man knew where he was a teacher at. Then he noticed the lanyard with the school's name and location hanging from his rearview mirror.

"Son, I can tell that you don't need to be doing this everyday if you are having panic attacks and stressing out like this. You're in Welcome, North Carolina—what part of North Winston-Salem are you trying to get to?"

"I don't live too far from the Lawrence Joel Coliseum, about three apartment complexes from Wake Forest University."

The man shook his head. "I tell you what, I'll follow you to the coliseum and trust that the Good Lord will lead you the way home."

Calvin turned on the engine and he slowly got back on the right lane and stayed on US 52 until he got to his exit. As he was thinking, he had considered whether if he wanted to move to Concord. The drive home would be easies but he was starting not to feel welcomed to teach there next year. The nit picking and negative reviews that Calvin recently received were just as worrisome as the two and a half, almost three hours Calvin spent on the road everyday. Some days the drive was longer if traffic was in bad shape and that cut into his own time.

Wes' conversation didn't leave him in a better position and he knew he had a lot to think about.

Chapter Twenty-Nine

Tuesday, November 18, 2008
Butler J. Parker Library
2:35pm

Calvin and Miguel attended a school-wide mentor/mentee meeting. They learned about different teaching strategies and defining what works and doesn't work in the classroom. Everyone was encouraged to submit an idea. Calvin talked about an idea that worked for two of his classes but didn't work as well as he wanted it to for another class. He described how he turned that idea around to make it something that the students in that class could relate to.

Miguel had spent quite of bit of time working with Calvin on his Individualized Growth Plan on improving as a teacher. Calvin had to redo his plan because Wes wanted him to incorporate some of the things he noticed in the review as part of the plan. The IGPs are modeled after the INTASC Standards that are posted on the North Carolina Department of Instruction website.

The classes had started on the new Spreadsheets unit. He was excited about using the Excel program because this would allow him to show the students how they could use the program at home in their "everyday life."

Calvin decided to teach the students how to budget their money. After he taught the basic concepts of a spreadsheet program, he was going to show them how to build and maintain an electronic check book. Prayerful that will encourage the students to make daily entries as they spent and received money. What he hoped would happen was that a few students see the negative effects of their spending habits and will be committed to making changes for the better.

Calvin spent time explaining to Miguel how he was excited to see what the students produced for their budget project. In all of the classes, Calvin noticed that some of them were talking about it and he prayed they notice the changes they could be making in their spending habits.

Even with the project not being part of the curriculum, he knew that half of the students may never take another business class again, either by choice or design. So Calvin wanted to use the opportunity to educate them and give them an opportunity to take something they learn in class and use it in real life.

Wes came into the room and took a seat next to Calvin. Calvin could see a change in the man immediately. Wes didn't greet him—didn't acknowledge his presence—and had been acting funky since Calvin didn't stay at that party that he knew in his spirit would cause him problems.

Once the meeting was over, Wes asked that Calvin and Miguel stay for a couple of minutes so they could go over the evaluation that Wes had given for his visit to Calvin's class the day before. They'd barely said more than two words to each other than either.

"Calvin, I think we have a problem," Wes started as the last of the teachers were leaving.

"Why you say that?" Calvin said.

"You are a boring teacher. You open the class with a video, then you talk about spreadsheets. Then you send the students to create some spreadsheets, you have them return to their desks to talk about spreadsheets some more. You are below standard in almost everything I evaluated you for."

"How can that be?" Miguel asked in disbelief. Miguel had done a surprise evaluation the Thursday before. "Calvin is moving through the class at a faster pace. He opens, introduces the topic, invites students to impart their knowledge, then they work on the example together and then he gives them an opportunity to work on the assignment on their own."

"Who is the API, me or you?" Wes snapped.

"I'm his mentor, I'm supposed to go to bat for him—especially since he's made dramatic improvements to his teaching style since he was here. Calvin's sacrificing almost everything in his life so that he can become an effective teacher."

"But I'm the boss—and point blank, Calvin sucks. Here is the evaluation. Bruh, if you don't step your game up, you won't be stepping foot on this campus anymore."

Calvin looked at the evaluation and gritted his teeth. He knew there were areas that needed improvement but he felt like Wes nit-picked everything Calvin could have done wrong and amplified it.

"This is some mess," Miguel looked at the evaluation. "I guess because you've held your ground about your faith—he's trying to punish you for it in your review."

"I figured as much. I didn't want to say it but I finally realized that you were telling me the truth."

"Nothing to feel bad about. I apologize for being right."

"I guess I need to start looking for another school to teach in or another job."

"Calvin that's too dangerous. I say focus on getting your education and try to pass the classes you are struggling in. Then everything else will take care of itself."

"Yeah."

"Sometimes, God himself is taking things away and removing people so that we can be completely focused on Him and what it is He wants us to do for Him. Now is not the time to give up the faith—now is the time to take a firm stand on it."

Calvin looked at the evaluation again and put it in the suitcase. He could feel his life changing but he wondered whether or not this was for the best.

Tuesday, November 25, 2008
Mr. Rice's Room
2:35pm

A few teachers had warned Calvin that many students took off Monday and Tuesday before the Thanksgiving holiday so that they could have a whole week off from school. The idea sounded crazy because the students already had a four-day weekend when they got off for Fall Break in October.

The students were going to do what they were going to do.

The sand colored box on Calvin's desk caught his attention. Calvin originally was just going to drop by the room, gather his prepared rolling bag and head to the mandatory impromptu meeting that was called.

"The janitor just dropped it off a few minutes ago,." Reverend Conseco said as she was gathering her things from his desk. Calvin quickly opened the box and noticed review copies of the new text books from SouthWestern. They weren't exactly new, he'd seen the books a year before at the school he'd done his field study in. He admired the Accounting book and wanted to take it home for leisure reading over the Thanksgiving copy. He'd wished that the books had come last semester when he was pitching the classes to the students and administration.

"If I didn't know any better, I'd say it was Christmas time."

Calvin chuckled and silently admitted to himself that Reverend Conseco was right.

"I love books and I love to write," Calvin admitted. "If given the opportunity, I'd like to contribute to writing one of the books or at least reviewing them in the future. Who knows, maybe that can be my next career move in addition to teaching—a published author in the business education field by the age of thirty-five."

"That's not a bad aspiration at all."

"Time to come to the meeting," Miguel said from the door way. Calvin grabbed a couple of the other business books as well as the rolling bag and followed Reverend Conseco out of the classroom. "I can't believe we are going to have a meeting before the Thanksgiving Holiday. I'm looking forward to a few days without students or dealing with the administration, even though I will spend most of the weekend grading papers and trying to get ahead for this last stretch."

"I'll be catching up on school work. Still trying to hang on to those classes." Calvin said. "I almost wished I had dropped out this semester but you know I don't like to quit anything."

"How is school going?" Reverend Conseco asked.

"Not good."

"Don't give up. You still got a final and some time to turn things around."

"Yeah, but my finals are in two weeks."

Calvin dreaded the thought that between worrying about his teaching job and going through his divorce that he might flunk out of grad school. But he pushed the thought to the back of his mind—wanting to spend the first Thanksgiving with his brother since they were children.

By time Calvin, Miguel and Reverend Conseco got to the cafeteria, it was standing room only. No bother to Calvin because that made it easier for him to leave.

Dr. Hewett was standing before the crowd tearful and in a somber mood.

"Greetings Staff…I won't be before you long. I just have a few announcements to make before we head out for the break."

A few teachers murmured and then quieted down.

"For one, I wanted to wish all of you a happy and safe Thanksgiving holiday. Next, I want to announce that I have accepted the principal position of the new Michael Jordan Academic Academy that they are building and will be open for the 2009-2010 school year."

Claps and murmurs could be heard throughout the cafeteria. Calvin didn't know what to think—the man whom tormented him would be leaving.

"I'm going to turn the rest of the meeting over to our superintendent Dr. Clarke Baxter."

Calvin watched as the elder, frail, but inspirational man stepped forward. As the man talked, he thought about how the news would affect him. Dr. Hewett would have a whole year to build a staff and an administration. The superintendent announced that they would post the vacancy for the principal's position today and that they would be considering all eligible candidates for the position.

Shortly after his announcement, the meeting was adjourned. Most of the teachers were disappointed and I noticed that a few of them congratulated him publicly on accepting the position. Their main discontent is that in the seven year history of Butler J. Parker High School, they've already had three principals and they did not want another one. On the other hand, since they have to have another principal and the superintendent said that "our thoughts" would be considered—some of the teachers have made it very clear that they want Wes lead them into the future.

Just as Calvin was getting ready to go after talking with some of the other teachers, Calvin saw Wes motioning for him to come his way. When Calvin got within arms' reach—he was handed a small piece of paper with an address on it.

"Wear something leisure—we got to hang out before the holiday. And some of the brothers will be there."

Calvin smiled and looked at the address. The residential address in Kernersville put him near his neck of the woods. Calvin really didn't want to be bothered with Wes, but decided that he'd go to keep the peace.

***

Calvin nodded his head as he heard Byron Cage's "Royalty" on The Light. He sang along and praised God in his brother's 2008 Honda Civic. Discarded wrappers from Chick-Fil-A and Burger King covered the smoky-colored mat on the floor. On top of that, toys from the kid's meal rode on top of the mess.

This is the last time I 'borrow' Carlton's car. I have got to get mine back soon. He thought about Carlton and his newfound desire to create a mess-capade. That man was too grown to be leaving trash all over the place.

As he redirected her focus on the road, Calvin thanked God for the pine mint air freshener that was working overtime to overpower the smell of fast food in the car. When Byron finished honoring God, Calvin wondered why he was agreeing to meet with Wes at some house party to begin with. He shook his head as he eased off the pedal and gently pressed the brake to come at a complete stop.

Calvin looked out of the passenger side and even though it was darker than midnight outside, he could tell by the profile of the girl driving the car beside him that she had to be fine. Her hair touched the roof of her car—whatever type it was and her frame was slender like a basketball player. He smiled even though he knew she couldn't see him.

A car honked twice and a lady's voice, who nicknamed herself Victoria because of her preppy and high-pitched tone interrupted his thoughts.

"Turn Right on Robinson in two blocks." Victoria had repeated twice.

"Man I heard you the first time." Calvin complained, knowing that the GPS system could not hear him or reply back.

Calvin finally moved the car and was ready to follow the directions Victoria gave him as he finally made his way to the estate the party was in. He saw the line of cars along-side the driveway and pulled in the next available spot. The chorus to Mary Mary's "God In Me" blasted over gospel rapper that had claimed the airways and Calvin felt his Blackberry vibrate in his pocket. Calvin reached into his pants, grabbed the phone and put it to his ear.

"Dude, is you here yet?"

Calvin couldn't believe that Wes was keeping track of him.

"Yeah man, I just got here."

"Hurry up and park—you already fifteen minutes late and you are about to miss the show."

"Aight." Calvin shook his head and pressed the END button to disconnect. He turned off the engine and got out of the car. He walked to the backseat and grabbed the casual shoes that were more comfortable and subtly checked himself to make sure he was right.

"Can you move a little quicker please?" The voice from behind him made him drop the shoes on the ground. Calvin clutched his fingers in a tight ball over his heart, hoping to contain its rapid pounding inside of his chest. He felt another panic attack coming on.

"Man you scared me."

"Well get unscared, every second you're out here is fun not had by either of us."

Calvin knew what Wes was saying was true. He noticed his boss's black slacks and solid red polo. His Rolex watch shined bright and complimented the neck piece that was hanging out of his shirt.

"Unbutton them buttons man and relax. We came to this house party to have fun and be around some other educated black men who need to unwind."

Calvin scrunched up his lips as Wes led the way. He was hoping that Wes wasn't trying to hook him up with any miscellaneous woman.

Calvin stepped into the house and noticed that the lights were dark with hues of red and black scatter. Smoke and the smell of scented tobacco floated through the air. A fully naked young lady walked to the room and came greeted them. Wes stepped in while Calvin stepped out.

"Man, you leaving again?" Wes gripped.

"Wes, I told you—this is not my kind of party. I'm not that kind of man anymore."

"If you'd unwind just a little bit, your students could relate to you better and you would be more popular."

"I don't want to be popular, I want to be right. I can't set a good example for the students if I'm out acting a fool."

"Man, get in this house, have a few drinks and settle down— your job is on the line and I'm trying to help you save it."

"Since when did being a teacher involve random sex parties, illicit drugs and dark lights?"

"Since the county and state started shoving all kinds of unrealistic mandates and other mess down our throats. This is the one time a week I can forget about being Mr. Johnson and wild out."

"I serve a God that gives me the comfort I need to unwind without having to compromise my body to do so."

"You go and take that Jesus with you. I'll have all the fun and tell you about it at our meeting."

The door shut and Calvin was disappointed that Wes had left him on the other side. He could hear Miguel's warning loud and clear and at that moment, he knew exactly what it meant.

Chapter Thirty

Calvin stepped into Wes's office and he knew what he was about to hear may not have been good. He said a silent prayer to God that either he'd get an extension or he would be able to bounce back quickly if he did in fact lose his job. In preparation for the later, he'd already put in applications with other school systems to become a substitute teacher and a direct care worker—positions he'd held before.

In his heart, Calvin knew he'd given the job 110% and that the work he'd done made an impact on the students he taught. He arrived to the classroom early and stayed late. He helped them reactivate the FBLA chapter. He always made himself available when one of the EC teachers needed him for a meeting. As Calvin took a seat across from his former mentor, former friend, he'd begun to pity him. He looked at the golden image of Buddha and shook his head. The statue seemed to stare at him as if it could see through him.

I rebuke you in the name of Jesus! Calvin's spirit boldly declared and the statue seemed to be less menacing. He saw the letters and the pictures glorifying their fraternity, but felt no brotherly love from the man who sat across from him. Of all of the administrators who led him to this moment, he was the worst. Calvin reaffirmed his reason for not wanting to let anyone get too close to him. Wes reminded him that people could not be trusted and when he finally took his seat, he felt the temperature in the room get forty degrees cooler. That's when he knew it was colder in Hell.

"Sup Bruh," Calvin heard him say. *Bruh*—he was far from that. Wes had violated in a major way and the last thing he should have been referring to himself was as someone's "bruh."

"Sup," Calvin replied in a low voice.

The tension in the room was thick. Calvin could hear Wes breathing and the old him—the side of him that wanted to murder without cause—do the very thing he hadn't done since he was twelve years old started to rise in him. Calvin noticed the solemn look on Wes's face—he didn't trust it. He felt like he was around a father who was getting ready to lie to his son.

"How are you doin'?"

Calvin hated the fact that Wes was trying to drag out the bull. *Just say what you want to say Satan and get the hell up out of my face,* Calvin thought. He knew that Satan was messing with him and that Wes was more than happy to be used by him. Satan, was the master procrastinator.

"You should've come with us to the mall," Wes said, attempting to lighten the mood. "My son and daughter were walking around, begging me to let them see Santa. My son asked for one of those talking Elmo toys. I wasn't feeling it because Elmo's not for boys, ya'know what I'm saying? But my wife surprised me and went ahead and got it. Then my daughter been on this Dora the Explorer kick and trying to speak Spanish and all of that—so daddy made sure she was taken care of too. Christmas can be so expensive—I think I spent about three hundred dollars on gifts for them so far."

Really, this dude is bragging about spending three hundred dollars on Christmas gifts—knowing that my children are dead and that I can't buy them gifts. Calvin tried to do the breathing technique that the anger management instructor had taught him but he could feel himself about to explode.

"I was talking with Kisa, the director of human resources—we had a dinner with some of the administrators and what have you. We talked about your assessments and the fact that you flunked out of grad school."

"Look, I don't want to waste anymore of my time," Calvin pulled out the envelope that had his resignation letter in it and handed it to Wes. He took his Butler High lanyard from around his neck and handed it to him. "All this bull about what you are doing for your children while trying to avoid the fact that you really want to let me know that I'm not going to have a job anymore is really disrespectful to me. I'll teach the rest of the semester like we agreed and then after January 29, you won't ever have to see me again."

Wes looked like he was about to choke. He let out a small cough and then tried to stand at his desk, "yo' are you serious?"

"Of course I am. You know something, when I told you I flunked out of my graduate program, I never said that I couldn't teach. And when I talked to one of the administrators in Guilford County, she already said all I had to do was to retake the one class I failed that was needed to clear my lateral entry license and find a school that would agree to sponsor me and give me another job."

"That's not we talked about." Wes was defensive. Calvin stood up because the last thing he wanted was for Wes to be looking down on at him.

"You mean that's not what you lied about—look. You got what you wanted. You schemed and you played me so that you could get what you wanted. You wanted me out of here and that's what you got."

Calvin headed to the door because he could feel that he was two seconds from punching Wes dead in his grill and the *last* thing he needed was for him to go to jail. He was meeting with the other Street Disciples to pass out devotions and inviting them to the nativity program that was being held at his church. Sure he could preach from prison, but Calvin had other ambitions and he couldn't do those things from prison.

"You know this means you can't come back right?" Wes sneered as a crooked laugh escaped his lips.

Keep me near the cross, Calvin asked Jesus as he wanted to plant his fist into Wes's jaw. Visions of Calvin breaking Wes's skull at the edge of the table flirted in his mind. He could hear Satan chanting "do it, do it," but decided he wasn't going to entertain those thoughts.

"I know two things—one is that Jesus Christ is Lord and two, I was not designed to live my life as the spec on the piece of gum on the bottom of someone's shoe.

"God bless you and your job man. I wish you the best." Calvin looked at Wes one last time and walked right out of his office. He saw the clock on the way out of the door and figured he had about an hour before he had to teach his next class. Miguel had requested that he'd come to his classroom and share the news with him either way.

Calvin walked down the hallway knowing his days at Butler J. Parker were numbered. He saw Dr. Hewett and Evelyn heading his way from some meeting. Evelyn appeared sad and looked away. Calvin realized that even though he felt disconnected from Evelyn, she was the administrator that had his best interest at heart. Evelyn was the one that cared about him.

Calvin looked at the clock and realized he had ninety minutes to get his class together. He decided to make the best of that.

***

Wednesday, December 17, 2008

Calvin's Bedroom
10:45 PM

Calvin was supposed to join Carlton at the Street Disciples prayer meeting and Bible study but decided that he couldn't take it. He didn't want to bother Rahliem or the rest of the guys with his teaching drama.

He picked up his bottle of Vodka and took a sip straight from the bottle. He'd been nursing the liquid from his locked room for a while.

No job—no school—only one more bad thing for Calvin and the saying would be true—bad things come in three.

Calvin heard his phone vibrate and the ringtone he had designated for Maria came on. He hadn't heard that Jesse Powell song in a long time.

R U UP? She asked.

Yeah. Calvin replied. *I wonder what she wants.* Calvin thought as he sat on the bed and took another sip of the alcohol.

R U @ Home?

Yeah.

Come open the door—I'm outside.

Huh? Calvin asked as he got up and unlocked the bedroom door. He walked to the door and heard a light knocking. He looked through the peephole and was surprised to find Maria on the other side. Calvin opened the door.

"I'm glad you're here." Maria said as she opened the door.

"What do you want—why have you come?"

Calvin looked at Maria, whose head was hanging down. "I want you."

"No you don't."

"No I'm serious. I messed up—I made a mistake, I want you."

Calvin was trying to hold her back but the liquor had begun to do its work and impair Calvin's mind, body and spirit. "I'm not interest—" Calvin couldn't even get the words out right. His mind made one decision—but his body had made another as he responded to her touches, yearning to join her in the way a husband is supposed to cleave to his wife.

Friday, December 19, 2008
Calvin's Bedroom
8:24 AM

Maria woke up and put on her clothes. She goes to her closet when she realized that she wasn't at her house. As she wiped her eyes and looked around and realized that she was in Calvin's apartment and she didn't have any clothes at the condo anymore.

She turned around and looked at the bed she had just shared with Calvin.

Thirty-six hours had passed and the two of them were in as much sin as Adam and Eve when they bit into that fruit.

I said I wouldn't sleep with him again. Maria thought as she searched for something she could wear that would do for the moment.

"What's wrong?" Calvin asked as he sat up in the bed. He looked down and grinned when he seen that he was wearing his wedding band and when he looked to see hers blinging on her finger, his smile got wider.

"This whole arrangement—me, you, this bed, your place. This isn't college you know."

Calvin fidgeted in his bed. "So what are you saying? You didn't enjoy sleeping with me last night." Calvin reached on the floor to find something to wear and finding nothing, he stood up, grabbed the sheets and wrapped it around his waist.

"We're divorced, Calvin."

"Not legally—and after what we did last night."

"Divorcing couples don't have sex." Maria interrupted.

"We just did—if I remember correctly, we've been in my bed since Wednesday night."

"Oh my God you're missing the point." Maria said as she snatched a NC Tech University sweatshirt from the hanger and forced it on her body. "I came over here to get a break from Bilal."

"A break? What is this?"

Clearly, Maria forgot about how she told Calvin that she loved him over and over again—how she made a mistake with Bilal and how she wanted to work things out. And Calvin, in his excitement didn't mind "working" things out in an effort to save their marriage.

"I messed up because I can see that I gave you the wrong impression. You believe that we still love each other."

"You don't love me?" Calvin was upset. He still loved her. Took her back even as he'd suspected that she'd been with Bilal recently.

"Not like that," Maria found her way into some of Calvin's sweat pants. "You know what I mean."

"I don't think I do."

There's a knock on the bedroom door.

"Who is that?" Maria rushed to fix her hair in the mirror. Calvin went to the bathroom to put on some clothes. When Calvin stepped out, he walked to the bedroom door and answered it.

"Carlton," Calvin said as he looked at his brother.

The smell of eggs and turkey bacon that Carlton was cooking made its way to their room. Maria rushed to the bathroom and ran the water.

"Oh—you and Maria are back together?" Carlton's eyes lit up in excitement. "I knew you was in here with someone. Glad it was her."

Calvin looked at his hand. His ring was a deception to the state of the situation he was in, yet, he didn't have the heart to take it off.

"Everything isn't as it seems bro. I'm just now learning that."

"It's going to take more than a couple of trips down memory lane and a couple of acrobatic trips to keep a woman. If she wants to stay with you then make a house for her—but if not, let her go and stop allowing your body to tell your heart lies."

"That's easier said than done," Calvin looked away.

Maria walked out of the bathroom. The Honey Cocomango Body Lotion from Dudley's exuded from her skin.

"I have a question for you." Calvin stepped to the side to let Maria pass. He knew what was going to come next, but he held his cool.

"Yo, what's up?" Maria said casually.

"Have you ever considered getting re-married?"

Calvin wanted the answer to be yes. If he could've proposed to her again, he would have.

"No—I want our divorce to go through—which means this will have to be the last time we connect on this level."

"Let her go," Carlton mumbled.

"Fine," Calvin watched as Maria walked down the hallway. She stopped to put on her shoes and pick up her clothes that Carlton had place on the side. Maria looked back and stepped out of the door.

"Let her go." Carlton said more clearly. "Go wash up and then meet me at the table to get some of that food and grab the Bible and I'll talk to you when we sit at the table."

Calvin went to the bathroom to himself together and Carlton went back to the kitchen.

...the hard way

Chapter Thirty-One

Sunday, November 20, 2010
Maria's Condo
Winston-Salem, North Carolina

Calvin exhaled.

It had been almost two years since he was forced to resign from his teaching job at Butler J. Parker High.

He never thought he'd be re-living his days as a teacher.

Even though the ride could be strenuous and time-consuming —he almost missed driving back and forth to Concord on a daily basis. He missed Miguel and had lost touch with him after the man retired last year. He even missed Charlie, Otis, Chante, Shad and the rest of the students.

A part of him wondered whether or not Wes found his way back to Jesus and turned away from his Buddhist god. Calvin remembered the undergrad days when Wes' voice could carry a Smokie Norful or Byron Cage or a Donnie McClurkin song from one end of the building to the next.

These days he wondered how many people were following Buddah and other like-minded people on the path to Hell.

A hand that found its way under his shirt brought him back to reality. He looked at Maria and gently removed his hand and put it in her lap.

"I can't do this tonight," Calvin stood up and stretched.

"Why not?" Maria pouted like a seven year old who dropped her candy on the floor.

"You know why."

"But I'm not married to Bilal yet."

Calvin shook his head, "but one day you will be."

Maria took to tickling Calvin's side, hoping to make him laugh. Get him excited enough to make him want to be intimate with her. Though Calvin let a grin slip on his face, he also took a couple of steps back.

"You promised me you'd take your clothes off," Maria reminded him as she continued to try to lift his shirt up.

"And I will," Calvin moved her hand away and pulled his shirt down, "at home. Once I step into the shower and retire for the night," Calvin reached into his pocket and pulled out his keys. "You watch the movie or read the book on the table to keep you company."

Calvin walked to the door and without looking back, he opened it and walked out of Maria's condo for the last time. He walked down the stairs and quickly entered his car.

Calvin had every reason to be proud that he resisted temptation.

Chapter Thirty-Two

Friday, November 18, 2010
Forsyth County District Court House
Winston-Salem, North Carolina

"Are you sure you wanna do this?" Bilal asked Maria as they sat in his black 2010 Nissan Maxima. She stared into his coffee colored eyes and was mesmerized by the way his eyes seemed to smile at her. Bilal grabbed her hand and interlocked it with hers as they laid it on the arm rest. Maria looked down at her French acrylic nails then looked at that smile.

"Yes!" She shouted, then she jumped out of the car in her cream colored Vera Wang evening dress that she had chosen for this moment. Bilal was tempted to get out of the car and run after her, but instead he watched those legs run up the ivory white steps and the matching Jimmy Choos pumps pound the slates as they made a rhythmic clapping sound. She turned back around. "Come on Bilal—we don't have all day."

Bilal tilted the rearview mirror and looked at the sky blue collarless shirt Maria had chosen for him. He made sure that his facial hair was on point, that his lips weren't chapped and he licked his index finger and made sure that his eyebrows and goatee were straight. Bilal didn't have one strand of loose hair on his face or neck—he was ready for his close up.

After checking the rearview mirror to make sure that there wasn't a car coming, Bilal stepped out and pressed the LOCK button on keyless remote. He lightly jogged to catch up to the woman that was moving her hands franticly to hurry him along. Maria had changed her mind several times and he wanted to make sure they said "I do" before she could change it again.

Bilal and Maria walked hand and hand into the courthouse, defying all common logic to have their wedding in a church. Maria always hated the idea of the big church wedding and she wanted something subtle and private. She didn't invite her foster mother and Bilal chose not to invite his non-supportive family. Bilal noticed that Maria had tilted her head downward and was staring off into space. He lifted up her chin and she smiled.

"Baby, everything is gonna be alright," Bilal assured her as they crossed the entrance into the courthouse. They looked more like they were going to a church service then saying our vows for the first time. After going through the body scanners, they were escorted into the room where the small service was going to be.

Looking at the short, tan colored judge with slanted eyes, a slight muscular build that contradicted the salt and pepper strands of hair made Maria almost wish she were walking down the aisle with him. Normally, she wasn't attracted to older men but the judge did manage to keep her attention.

"I'm not late am I?" Pastor Goodwill turned heads as he made his entrance in the room. Bilal smiled at the man who was close in age to his father—even though he looked like one of the boys. Pastor Goodwill's bald head managed to shine and his brown sugar features complimented the peach button up and the black and orange tie that he wore with black slacks.

Maria should've felt guilty looking at this man of God and licking her lips. She wished she could do things with him and her soon-to-be husband at the same time.

Bilal had asked him a few days ago if he would agree to come to the courthouse with them. He hadn't been to Pastor Goodwill's church in over two years, but he knew that the man supported him as he looked to expand his ministry and his work with helping former ex-cons assimilate back into society.

"No sir," the Justice of the Peace spoke up in a barely audible baritone, "you're right on time. Stand beside the groom, please."

Maria smiled as the Egyptian Musk oil penetrated her air space. She was tempted to leave Bilal in the room by himself as she struggled to contain the lust for both the pastor and the justice of the peace. "I do." Maria spoke up, surprising herself by taking her mind out of the gutter and focusing on the ceremony.

"I do." Bilal said, binding himself to Calvin's ex-wife forever. The last five years of being "Boyfriend #2" as Pleasure P called it, had been a gift and a curse. The gift because he genuinely loved Maria and wanted to spend the rest of his life with her. Bilal felt that he could help her get to know Christ and give her life to him and that by living together as husband and wife, Bilal could provide her a better example. The curse because Bilal never pictured sharing his name with a woman who had been married before.

"I now pronounce you husband and wife, you may kiss your bride."

Bilal and Maria wasted no time expressing their passion for one another. Bilal blinked his eye open and saw the reaction on Pastor Goodwill's face and immediately slowed his roll. The courthouse was not the appropriate place for him to consummate his marriage.

"Well," the Justice of the Peace choked up, "let's sign the marriage license and you guys can be on your way handling that."

Once Maria signed the license and the paperwork making her Mrs. Kodjoe, everything they did from that moment forward was no longer sin. Bilal was glad that he had brought his black American Express card because he decided on a whim to have them check into the Marriott across the street, rent out their best suite and tame the beast that threatened to overtake him. Pastor Goodwill shook their hands and invited them to come to his church on Sunday so he could congratulate them in front of the congregation. Bilal was happy to have support from one of his boys on the biggest day of his life.

"I'll race you to the hotel," Maria challenged as they walked out of the door and down the steps of the courthouse. Bilal gave her a five second head start, looked both ways, and then crossed the street to claim his prize.

Sunday, December 20, 2010
Winston-Salem, North Carolina

Bilal seemed to be able to do the impossible—Maria was sitting next to him in his usual row in the middle of the church. He didn't have to usher or preach today and other than doing his part to collect the tithes and the offerings, he was happy to be in the presence of the Lord, and to have his wife at his side.

The chandelier that hung from the twenty two foot high ceiling always captivated him and held his attention. The choir was singing "Faithful is Our God" by Hezikiah Walker and he was singing along. Maria looked at him like he was crazy but Bilal had faith that one day, Maria would understand.

Bilal loved this song and how it made him feel, even on his worst day. His eyes subtly moved to the soloist—Lyla, that was her name. She had them baby face features that would bring any man weak to his knees.

He felt bad looking into her eyes as she sang out for the Lord and for a moment in time, he wished they could relive their early days as college sweethearts. He saw the wedding band on her finger and was reminded of the one on his.

They were together until Bilal ran into Maria again after not seeing her since his high school days. He couldn't remain faithful to Lyla because he wanted her and Maria too, and Lyla wasn't about to have that.

Before Bilal became a deacon, he would try to woo and chase after Lyla and she always seemed to make a conscious effort to avoid being in the same space as Bilal for longer than a few seconds. Even when she was seeing the man she ultimately married—something in his gut told him that the "real" reason she was avoiding him was one of two things: A—Lyla loved her man and was struggling not to cheat; B—she really was doing what she said she was doing and Bilal was too big of a temptation for her.

Bilal was too prideful to ask or beg for a level of companionship that he could get freely from the next woman. But he hated looking in her eyes. Even sitting with his wife beside him, he couldn't stop thinking about what it would be like if he had stayed with Lyla instead.

A smooth licorice-colored lady wearing *M* by Mariah Carey made her way to the podium to make the Sunday announcements. Bilal could tell she was wearing a lace front because her hair was way too shiny and had too much shine on it for it to be hers. It bounced and flung as if it belonged on one of the black Barbie dolls sold at the Dollar Store. She walked with a small pep in her step and she took her time as if the whole world was waiting on her to make some big, grand announcement. He and Maria looked at each other and shared a knowing smile at the inside joke they had about her.

"Good mourn-ing church." She said as she worked her head like a bobble head. Bilal hid a smirk knowing that God didn't like ugly and he had promised to refrain from acting a fool in His church. "I'm Sister Ernestine Maybelle, and I have the church a-nounce-ments for the day. Oh yes, Lord."

While Bilal kept his promise to behave, he made note of the couple in front of them who struggled to contain their laughter.

"We have some joys, this morning."

"Yes Lord!" Bilal hated when Barbara Lee jumped in the air and began her show. Every time Sister Ernestine said 'we had some joys,' Barbara Lee took that as her cue to be the unofficial co-host of the Sunday news.

"Joy numba one." Sister Ernestine danced around like that old lady from *Sanford & Son* and bobbled her head again. "Cedric Ho, was asked to co-write that gangsta rapper DaSite's novel."

A light applause could be heard as Bilal looked around to see if Cedric had even made the service. Bilal didn't see him but he did see Pastor Goodwill get up and take the newspaper clipping she had read from.

"Oh Lord, Jesus, forgive me. I apologize for making that announcement in front of the congregation. I brought it with me so I could ask him about writing a book on my life since he writing books and all. Well, praise God Cedric still has a job.

"Next announcement—haha—I'm reading from the right page now, thank you Jesus. Cedric and Aiesha are engaged to be married and their son is going to have his Christening at the church next month."

That was an announcement to clap for. Bilal finally caught him near the back holding his son over his right shoulder concealed in pure white sheets. Aiesha stood beside him looking like a high school cheerleader wrapping her arms around his. They waived at the congregation and the congregation waved back.

Sister Ernestine grunted and everyone turned to face the front. Then she plastered a smile that look like she had been attending clown school. "Next a-nounce-ment." She broke the word down as if it pained her to say it correctly. "Pastor Goodwill

will be graduating from the University of Chicago with a Doctorate of Divinity. You go ahead Dr. Goodwill."

The church stood in applause. Bilal didn't even know Pastor Goodwill was still in school or making trips out of town. He must have taken care of his scholarly duties over the weekend.

"And, Lyla from the choir graduated from Virginia Tech two weeks ago with a bachelor's degree in mechanical engineering and will be continuing her studies at North Carolina A&T this summer."

Another round of applause—Bilal was tempted to see if he could cheat on his wife but chose not to. Sister Ernestine choked again and everyone turned around. "And another news. A congratulations for Mr. & Mrs. Aurice and Serita Evanovich on their recent marriage—recent marriage!"

Bilal's mouth dropped and the look on Maria's face was priceless. How she gonna read their announcement as if there were a problem.

"Judson hasn't been in the ground a full six months and already this hussy is on to the next one. How are y'all gonna be married?" She asked as she looked those small beady eyes into the crowd. Everyone in the church seemed to be looking for Aurice and Serita.

Bilal saw the looks of disapproval and disappointment—he was glad that he was not led to announce in front of the whole church that he and Maria had eloped as well And knowing Aurice, he knew the boy was struggling to contain himself and not set it off in God's house.

Bilal finally saw them on the other side of the aisle. It hurt his feelings to see the tears creeping from her eyes. The three boys looked shock with their eyes open wide and their mouths forming perfect O's. Pastor Goodwill escorted Sister Ernestine from the podium but the damage was done. Bilal knew that he and Maria had got married fast and that they didn't invite everyone, but he'd never expect the church to openly disapprove of anyone's union.

"Let's go," Aurice could be heard saying as he stood up and escorted Serita out of the pew. Judson Jr., James and Julian followed as they still were in shocked. Some of the other parishioners turned around but a few were watching us, awaiting our reaction.

Bilal was proud to see that Aurice was not going off on Sister Ernestine, giving her a heart attack right where she stood. Aurice had been working on his temper for years but Bilal thought things finally clicked when Aurice became a father. Once their family was out of their seats, Aurice held Serita's head as she lightly sobbed on his arm and led his family out of the church. A few people were heard trying to apologize but Aurice shoved them off.

Bilal got up so that he could at least meet them at the exit. Bilal finally caught up with them before Aurice got in the car.

"Yo man," Bilal tried to apologize.

"Save it," Bilal barely got two words out of his mouth before Aurice cut him off. "I didn't kill Judson and I wish for once that people would stop saying I did. If I wanted to kill him to get to Serita, I'd done it years ago."

Bilal knew what he meant.

"Don't give up on the church. Sister Ernestine was wrong and she will apologize."

"No need," the venom in Aurice's voice hurt Bilal to the core, "I'm through with this place. It's time for us to find another church home."

Bilial watched as Aurice pulled off. Just as Bilal turned around —he saw Maria talking to an older man right outside the church door.

Sunday, December 20, 2010

Entry to Church.

"It's been a long time Maria," Dr. Alvarez said as he gently grabbed her arm.

"I thought you were dead," Maria admired the older beady-eyed man.

"Impossible," Dr. Alvarez lifted up his hat, "I see you run through quite a few men."

"Excuse me?"

"What happened to the light-skinned one you were married to?"

How did he know? Maria started to question.

"Don't think I haven't been keeping track of you or your little love triangle. But that doesn't matter now. You have bigger issues to worry about. A certain man of royalty is looking for you and has been for some time. He is very close to finding you."

"Then why haven't you told King where I'm at?" She addressed her first love and baby's father by name. Saying it brought back the pain of losing their son the way she had to memory.

"Because I enjoy watching him sweat," Dr. Alvarez smirked, "and besides, the chase is good for him."

Maria shook her head. She knew King was a dangerous man when she met him—and she risked her life and left behind the only child she'd ever given birth to in order to get away. The last thing she wanted was to be caught up in some mess King was involved in and lose her life. Taking King, Jr. would have been a risk for her and the last thing she wanted was a fight with King she knew he couldn't win.

"So when are you going to tell him where I'm at?"

"I'm not crazy—I'd have to kill him. And right now, he makes me too much money to do that. But what I will say is that the game you are playing is bound to get you hurt. And *when* not *if, when* King finds you—you better pray to God he's a changed man."

"I didn't know you believed in God," Maria tried to change the subject.

"I'm an atheist," Dr. Alvarez boldly declared, "I am God."

Maria shook her head. She remembered the day Dr. Alvarez got shot like it was yesterday. If he was a god, he must not have been a good one. She saw Bilal approaching and she wanted to end the conversation before her new husband got too close. "I got to go."

"I'll let you go," Dr. Alvarez said as he lowered his hat over his eyes. "But you need to figure out what you are going to do/say to make things right with King. And maybe you should find out how Junior has turned out."

Maria watched as Dr. Alvarez and Bilal walked past one another—Dr. Alvarez to the small blue Jaguar that he illegally parked in the handicap spot and Bilal on his way back in the church.

"Who was that?" Bilal asked as he wrapped his arm in hers and escorted Maria back in the church.

"The spawn of Satan—he's not worth dealing with."

"Oh—do I need to han—"

"No," Maria almost shouted. "Let him walk away—please—just let him walk away."

Bilal and Maria walked back into the church and could hear the choir singing a Smokie Norful song. Maria turned around quickly to catch a glimpse at Dr. Alvarez and turned around just as fast.

The wicked smile only confirmed what she was thinking. She knew from that moment on her life, as well as that of Bilal's was in danger.

Chapter Thirty-Three

Monday, December 21, 2010
Calvin's New Condo
North Charlotte, North Carolina

Calvin and Carlton were unpacking the boxes that were spread all over Calvin's new condo near uptown Charlotte. The new 1600 square foot condo was newly painted a calming egg nog color and was complimented with mocha and crème sofa and love seat in the leaving room. The words "live happily, love always, laugh always" were painted with dark chocolate letters on the wall leading to the kitchen. Pictures of the last super and a black angel with her fingers pointing to the sky surrounded the living room.

Calvin found the box with his sheets and toiletries in them and headed to his new master bedroom. The king size mahogany frame was fitted with the spring board and the mattress. He put the box down and pulled out 1500 thread count Egyptian cotton sheets and fitted and made his bed military style. Carlton walked in as Calvin was hanging up the pure white curtains.

"Man this place is nice!" Carlton complemented as he took note of the 52" plasma screen television that hung on the wall opposite of the bed. He leaned on the dresser that was television. "You've really come along way since the teaching and the divorce."

Calvin faced his brother, "it was nothing but God. All I had to do was what He asked me to do and I was well on my way."

Calvin thought about the direction he had been given to leave Winston-Salem and to relocate to Charlotte and he smiled. He remembered the small apartment he moved into shortly after the divorce was final and the job he was able to secure with the Sprint call center. He worked there a few months until he was able to get the cash from his pension that he had saved while working for the state. Once he was able to cash it, God had put a vision on his heart to open a faith themed organic store in the middle of Charlotte's NoDa Arts district on North Davidson Street. The store, which he was directed to call Daniels, featured Christian fiction novels, faith themed literature and art, organic products and a small café. The strong faith based community in Charlotte and the surrounding areas as well as a portion of the black community became local customers and the store was appreciated for being Christ centered. While some of the other stores struggled here and there, Daniels thrived not just because of the store, but because Calvin worked with other store owners in the area and he planned faith themed events with some of the local churches and faith leaders in the community. The sales were enough for Calvin to buy a new 2010 Ford Focus and the condo valued at $150,000 for a $128,000 in cash.

Calvin never owned up to being a millionaire but he had invested in the store wisely and he had impeccable customer service which kept the store busy due to great deals and word of mouth. He partnered with many churches in the area to promote literacy, youth programs and as head of the Charlotte chapter of The Street Disciples Ministry, he continued to do the work he felt called to do.

"I want to go on a drive," Calvin said all of a sudden. Carlton was still unpacking some of the toiletries in the master bathroom.

"Drive where?" His voice echoed as if he were on a sound stage.

"I need to go somewhere." Calvin left the living room and he grabbed his lightweight jacket and put it on as he walked to the door. He stepped into his black, red and grey Jordan CMFT Max 12s that were by the door. I pulled out the remote to his black 2010 Nissan Altima and pressed the unlock button.

"We still got a lot of stuff to put up man, you know I'm not gonna help you…"

"Man, just get your shoes on and let's go."

Calvin and Carlton stared at each other for a minute, but both men decided to avoid confrontation. Carlton walked to the doorway and put on his old school red and white Converses and followed Calvin out of the door.

Calvin took out the remote and pressed the UNLOCK button and he got in on the driver's side. Once Carlton was situated, they left the condo and found themselves riding on University City Parkway/NC-49. The local gospel station was bumping Mary Mary's new song, "Walking." Calvin continued to go north on the street and was surprised to find out he was in Harrisburg again.

"Truthfully, I shouldn't have given you a hard time because I don't even want to do this, but I feel the Spirit leading me in this direction, so I'm going."

Calvin remembered the back roads that lead to Concord and to Butler J. Parker High School as if he were a native. As he got closer to the school, he closed his eyes for a quick minute and said a prayer, asking for peace and solitude. Calvin pulled up to the teacher's parking lot, shut off the engine and sat still.

"So this is where it all went down?" Carlton asked as he unlatched his seatbelt.

"Yeah."

Carlton got out of the car and walked to the front of the building. Calvin looked around and saw a few other cars in the parking lot. Most cars were parked on the student lot near the gym. A few buses from neighboring counties and as far away as

Wake County were lined up at the end of the lot. Calvin knew that Butler J. Parker was hosting its annual wrestling tournament. Calvin got out of the car too and once he felt his feet land on the concrete, he felt a bubbling in his stomach, then all of a sudden, the weight of the world seemed to lift off of his shoulders.

As Calvin walked to the door, he remembered Dr. Hewett, Charlie and Austin. He thought he could hear Austin calling after him once he pulled for the door and realized that the door was locked on a Saturday.

"Wonder what the Spirit wanted with you?" Carlton asked as they began walking around the campus.

"I don't know yet, I just knew He called for me to come here and I am trying to be obedient."

Calvin gave Carlton an informal tour of the school, pointing out different parts of the building and telling stories about some of the students he had taught there. They peaked inside the packed gymnasium and witnessed one of the school's students getting taken down and him tapping out. Calvin shook his head. They then walked around to the back of the school where Calvin point out some of the kids had made to the Speedway and they ended up to the window where his former classroom 702 stood. Calvin was surprised to find the blinds open and he walked to the window to take a peek inside. He saw the twenty four desks were still in the middle and that newer computers lined the walls. He saw that the new teacher had left the projector on, and unless someone was in the building, the light would be out by time they started their first class Monday morning. After looking inside for a few minutes, Calvin walked to the car.

Carlton had followed him silently as he made his way through the school, "your old classroom looks nice."

"Yeah…I wish I had a chance to say goodbye to the janitors before I left. They really looked out for me."

Carlton nodded his head. Calvin got in the car and he pushed START so that the ignition would start.

"I realize something," Calvin said as he put his seatbelt on. "I came here because I wanted to become a teacher and I wanted to make a difference in other people's lives. Since I opened Daniel's, I've made a difference in other people's lives. I needed a new car, and I got it, without this job. I wanted to get my master's degree and this Spring, I will get it, without this job. I wanted to own my own place and I've accomplished that, without this job. When I left here, I let these people think they could take my world and ruin it. But I realize that my world wasn't theirs to control—it was God's. Everything I wanted to accomplished, I did it in His time when he saw fit to make it happen for me. I didn't need this job to make me a better man or to accomplish this thing, all I needed was Him." Calvin backed out of the parking lot and he took one last look at Butler J. Parker High School, then he drove off and headed towards his new home and new life in Charlotte. "I came back so God could heal me and remind me that everything was going to be alright. And so that I could see that my life after this school has turned out just fine."

"I'm glad to hear you say that." Carlton said as he turned on the radio. 21:03's new song was on the radio and he smiled. "So are you at peace?"

"You bet I am."

Calvin let the PAJAM track delight his ears and happy thoughts of his future and moving forward with Christ began to take a permanent residence in his mind.

The Testimony

When I was forced to resign from my teaching job at the end of 2008, God placed it on my heart to write this book. Originally, *Broken But I'm Healed* was going to be a teen anthology I did as Jarold Imes that was to include short stories with other authors.

But God made it clear that He wanted me to use this title to tell this story and let it go.

I tried following His directions for the first two days after the revelation was given to me—I found my teaching journals and cut and pasted the good, bad and ugly experiences I had in the classroom and from my studies. I also wrote a chapter and outlined part of the book.

But when the reality of losing my dream job that I enjoyed set in—I found that I didn't have it in my heart to continue reliving my life as a teacher and I didn't want to write this book God told me to. The fact that I had been lied to and deceived by some of the very teachers and principals I trusted—not to mention that I flunked out of my alma mater's teaching program with no possibility of returning—and while we elected a president that gave us a lot of HOPE, I was getting ready to struggle to find a job that would even pay half of what I was making as a teacher— I didn't see God blessing me in this way. I was caught up in self and how I was feeling. I struggled to get my ideas together and to follow the original outline I'd set out for this story. I was so mad, so hurt and at the point of wanting to try to commit suicide again —and I almost did until I heard a small voice in my head—and that voice said vent.

And vent, I did. I met with someone who reminded me that I enjoyed writing adult romances and erotica that would make some of you blush. That I was good at it and at one time, made a decent amount of money doing it. Never mind the fact that I really should've put more effort into re-editing what was *He Changed the Game* and to have faith to follow the walk God had set up for me to be in both the young adult and the faith fiction markets. Forget that I had other Christ-minded stories that I wanted to write and had been called to tell. I tried writing those books but I was too far gone to focus.

I wanted quick healing but I traded one bad habit for another.

To avoid the pain and the hurt—and to force the thoughts I had of hurting myself out of my system, I didn't turn to Christ—I turned to the one habit I thought would make me happy—sex. I was young, single, accustomed to making a certain amount of money and I wanted to have fun. I avoided living the life of a bachelor for so long and I decided I wanted to "act my age." So sex and porn allowed me to return to a genre I hadn't written in six years. I had told God after I got saved that I'd never write erotica again but writing about sex was all I could think about and all I could finish. So my promise to God went out of the window and the first book would be born and then after a few months, another would be born and I'd help three authors craft another and encourage them to do more and then I gave ideas and words for another for another author and then I'd write the first sequel I'd ever written for one of my original creations and then I'd write another book that would become a cult classic. And then I'd ghostwrite a couple of more that talked about—sex, money, drugs, mayhem and self-gratification.

Sure, faith fiction was on the back of my mind—and thankfully God the father, His Son nor the Holy Spirit would not let me forget my assignment.

From early 2009 to late 2010—I couldn't listen to a Kirk Franklin, Mary Mary, Dave Hollister, Kiki Sheard, Donnie McClukin, Hezekiah Walker, Kurt Carr, Yolanda Adams or Patti LaBelle song without trembling. And you know those artists knew how to stay on the Gospel and classic R&B stations. And heaven forbid, "Broken But I'm Healed" by Byron Cage come across the airwaves, I'd break down in tears. And that song would come on all the time too—I swear I thought I heard it on the hip hop station I was listening to at the time. I'd be in my car doing work for my job or at a friend's house or in church or on my way to be with the lady I'd have no business being with, and if "Broken But I'm Healed" would come on, I'd cry. And I'm not talking tear drops—I would break down and almost fall out like I'd broken my leg or experienced the loss of a loved one.

But I had broken my heart—and was too prideful to accept that I was out of the will of God. I thought going to church would take care of my extra-sinful-activities but I was wrong.

I'd remember all the hurt and pain that I went through and I'd struggle financially with whatever I was dealing with too. This went on for almost two years until finally, I'd heard the song and I told the Lord, "Yes! I will write this book." Next thing I knew, the tears stopped, my vision was clear and I had a desire to make Isaiah David Paul more successful than Jarold Imes, Donte Sweat and Cedric Quincy and a few other names I legally can't disclose had been.

For the whole month of October 2010, I'd diligently went about doing His Will and crafted a sizable portion of this book. I remembered Calvin, whom I originally introduced in *Worth Fighting 4* by Jarold/Jaeyel Imes (I'm reprinting this book under Isaiah David Paul on Black Friday 2012) and decided to make a street disciple in *The Triumph of My Soul* and *Soul of a Man* and knew this was his story. I had just completed a draft of *Street Disciples* and knew I wanted to do more with Calvin. I remembered the 10,000 plus words that went beyond the request Elissa Gabrielle had for *Soul of a Man* and used that as the basis for this story. She encouraged me, called upon me to write this book—and to do what the Lord had commanded me to do. Others who participated in the anthology also held me accountable and we celebrated when I added a word or completed a sentence.

But then I got distracted and deceived again by a few people whom I'd thought were good people in Charlotte. At first, I didn't want to be bothered because I lost my teaching job in a county near Charlotte. But an offer to expand my business seemed like I could meet another dream and one I thought would further all of my visions so I put the book down to expand my business and made the biggest mistake of my life. I lost almost everything trying to help someone whom I thought was a friend have his dream and mine too. A man who lied about being a Christian just so he could keep his faith-filled customers in his store—customers who truly believed he was saved just because he attended a few church services at various places and would allow Christian organizations to have events in his store.

It seemed like every time I experienced some level of success, this man would get jealous of me. His new business partners and some of his friends who also weren't Christians hated me and they made sure I knew how they felt. And I have to say God and those whom I was close to in the literary industry all tried to warn me that I was doing business with Satan. An author whom I and many in this industry had great respect for put him on blast and I tried diligently to patch their relationship—didn't work. Others would warn me when I did my tour that year that I was in trouble and that this man wasn't whom he said he but I didn't listen. I had made so much money with this man in the past that I couldn't see what others clearly saw. All I could see was my dream and how I wanted to do all of these things for God and how I could live my dream as an entrepreneur and possibly get back into teaching.

Fortunately, I received a final warning that I couldn't ignore and before summer could come around, I walked out the day before I got my master's degree at Western Carolina. I didn't get to enjoy walking across the stage in peace because my former friend and business partners tried to have me arrested. They harassed and threaten me and my family—slandered my name on many social media sites. And they set about ruining my credit using the tools I'd helped them acquire.

And it wasn't just ruining my credit with a store that in hindsight I now realize I had no business being part of—it was also ghostwriting, not one but three projects that I never fully got paid for. I'm owed thousands of dollars for ghostwriting work and when you combine that with the losses I took from the store I'm still paying for, that's how I lost my last business.

In December 2011, after evaluating everything and doing a job that would lead to me creating a character in an upcoming anthology I will be in, I finally got to work finishing *Broken But I'm Healed*. God showed me where he would allow me to go and what I'd written that could be used in this book. God allowed me the next five months to get this book together while struggling to work a job I didn't like and to grow in a church where He'd want me to get nourishment from. God showed me the business I could have with Solomon Waterwine and what all I could do with it. He showed me how, even though I lost Abednego's Free and my books went out of print how He would help me bring them back. And that in His timing, I will be where I need to be to complete the mission He has especially for me.

God has shown me that I may have been broken, but I can heal with Him. I thank Him for allowing me to come back after I have messed up time and time again. I thank Him for placing it in my heart to forgive all my enemies and to move forward. To create works for Him again. I thank Him for allowing me to enjoy being a writer again. For the love I have for the Imes, Tinsley, Phelps, Simmons, Braggs, and Carter families. I thank Him for Barbara S. Grovner, Elissa Gabrielle, Loraine Elzia, Zeniah Latoude-Stevens and K. Roland Williams for the works they've done with this novel along the way.

And finally, I thank Him for you—for deciding to give a young country boy who loves God a chance to live his dream. I am the gritty Christian fiction writer with a secular past that ultimately wants to do His will. And while I won't promise that I won't mess up again or that I won't write secular books again (I've learned my lesson with that), I will say that I will strive to stay on the course and fight the good fight of faith.

That's what the Saints do after all—and Lord willing, when that day comes, I'll get to march with them.

About the Author

Over the years, Isaiah David Paul has written in a variety of genres and became a writing partner and ghostwriter for a few award-winning and best-selling authors. With his string of successes and renewed faith in God, Isaiah David Paul has finally decided to follow his calling to write under his own name. He has a business management degree from North Carolina Agricultural & Technical State University, a Masters of Entrepreneurship from Western Carolina University and a MAT-Elementary Education from the University of North Carolina at Greensboro. He is the author of over fifty titles under various pseudonyms and has contributed to the publication of nearly two hundred books. He lives a private life with his family in the Southeast United States.

Follow Isaiah David Paul on Social Media:

Official Website	IsaiahDavidPaul.com
Instagram	@IsaiahDavidPaul
TikTok	@IsaiahDavidPaul
Blue Sky	@IsaiahDavidPaul
Facebook	@IsaiahDavidPaul
Linktree	@IsaiahDavidPaul
X/Twitter	@IsaiahDavidPaul

www.ingramcontent.com/pod-product-compliance
Lightning Source LLC
Chambersburg PA
CBHW061614170626
46811CB00001B/428